T0328531

this day

DISCLAIMER:

This is a work of fiction. While the book is set
in the real town of Mossel Bay, all characters are
from the author's imagination. While the author
has been fairly true to the landscape, layout and
politics of the town, this is not a guidebook.
Certain fictional elements have been inserted
along with bending-of-reality(s) for both artistic
reasons and privacy.

First published by Modjaji Books (Pty) Ltd 2014
PO Box 385, Athlone, 7760, Cape Town, South Africa
www.modjajibooks.co.za

Copyright ©Tiah Beautement 2014
ISBN 978-1-920590-59-8
e-book ISBN 978-1-920590-85-7

Book and Cover Design by Megan Ross
Cover artwork by Tammy Griffin
Editor: Karen Jennings
Cover photo by CM Beautement

Printed and bound by Megadigital, Cape Town
Set in Garamond

this day

TIAH BEAUTEMENT

modjaji books

For Celie Eales an⬧ Ntombizo⬧wa Kokwe

Kai: earth (Scandinavian), sea (Hawaiian), fire (Scottish), forgiveness (Japanese)

MORNINGTIDE

The water devours the words.

A solid half hour of writing in the starlight, the sharp stick gouging the glassy sand, until it resembled a pewter tablet bearing prophecy. Moses would have been impressed. Now my work has nearly vanished, the water sucking the letters until they pop out and drift away.

The tide has changed, precisely when the tide table said it would. My mind cannot comprehend how they predict the ocean's behaviour so far in advance. I've had it explained to me, this gravitational pull between the sea, the moon and the sun. But life has so many variables – solar flares, falling stars, an unexpected gust of wind – how do the tides keep ticking by on schedule, as if these anomalies have not occurred?

Low tide: 4:59am.

This is what the pamphlet said.

That is what happened.

Dawn whispers in as the ocean surges forward. My stomach rolls and my flesh prickles as the surf collects around my ankles, combing through my toes. I remain planted, waiting for the sun.

'Ashes to ashes, dust to dust.' An often-spoken sentiment at funerals. I should know; I've been to enough. But in truth, we are mostly water: around sixty-to seventy-percent, if the experts are to be believed. They say an adult should drink two litres of water a day in order to maintain the approximately forty litres that compose the individual. I, Ella, am water. My words are somewhere in these waves, coating my feet. I should not be afraid. This sea contains droplets that were once in me, in my son, that sustained us both.

The sky grows brighter. There are no surfers out on dawn patrol. Not the right kind of waves. They are small and crumbly. Perhaps later today this will change. I used to be more aware of the surf report. Bart, my husband, had scheduled his days around it. Now my daily excursions to the beach are made alone, in silent homage to our beloved boy. Perhaps words reach us, even in death.

A barefoot fisherman in tatty trousers and a rusty red t-shirt approaches. A weathered plastic carrier bag dangles from calloused fingertips. His hooked knife glints in the dim light. He pays me no notice. We've seen each other often enough. I don't know his name, nor he mine. But like the rocks along the shore, we have become part of one another's scenery.

With slow deliberate steps, he works his way to the rocks where the mussels cling. The water continues to swirl about my ankles, at times brushing up against my calves. The sun's rays grow stronger. They reach out and lick my face. Soon the fisherman has wandered out of my line of vision. I do not turn my head. I wait and watch until the sun has finished emerging from the sea.

The interior of the Prius is cool, promising, as cars often feel in the early hours. By noon the cabin air will be stale, tired with disappointment.

Every day we begin again.

This day is no more significant than the one before, or the one before that. Little progress, if any, seems to be made. Yet, I keep trying, pushing, as if working towards something, even if that something cannot be named. What is it that I hope to gain? It would be easier to succumb to the endless cycle. I could crawl into bed and lie next to Bart. With a sigh, whisper his full name, 'Bartholomew,' as I welcomed the rot. Gradually, we would waste away. It is, after all, not without precedent. Then death would claim us, as it did his mother. Yet, even now, I can't help but think of it as the cowardly way out.

Making my way up Church Road, heading home, the sun rises steadily behind me. We do not live far from the sea. The walk would do me good. But Bart insists that I drive. I have yet to inquire what shadows he envisions stalking me on the Mossel Bay streets. He believes me safe in our home, surrounded by palisade fencing. He believes me safe on the beaches, no matter the hour. How, after all of this, can he continue to have such trust around a large body of water?

'You never go deeper than your ankles,' he says.

In the past I would have argued his odd logic, pointing out the holes. Or I might have ignored his protests entirely and simply walked. But the fact that he can muster the energy to insist on anything is… something.

We all need something.

*

Returning, I make my way down the hall, studiously ignoring the door to the main bathroom. We have yet to arrange for repairs. As far as I am aware, the antique bathtub remains in ruins – cast iron marred by the sledgehammer, shattered porcelain pooling at the base of clawed feet.

Stepping into the master bedroom I locate Bart, wrapped in a quilt, exactly as I left him. A line of drool channels along a heavily shadowed cheek. His ashy blond curls are overgrown and greasy. His once bronzed skin resembles spoilt yoghurt, the white separating into transparent layers that are tinged with blue. But it is the rhythmic rise and fall of his thin chest that holds my attention. Alive. This is never guaranteed. Each time I venture out of the house provides an opportunity to bring himself to conclusion. Despite everything, I do not wish for his death. I fear it. Anticipate it. Because I no longer understand what motivates him to exist. Gradually he has released us all from his care. Even his art.

His art was the last to go. In the past sixteen months, only two pieces have been created. The first was a glass box in blues, greens, and purples so dark they almost looked black. The colours drift together, echoing the sea's calm before the storm. The silver lines where the sections were soldered together give the box a distinctly religious overtone. We are not religious. But there is comfort in the aura of solemnity, given its contents.

The other piece is a glass blown sculpture, unlike any of the vases, bowls, platters, Christmas ornaments and cut glass jewellery that he, or his three partners, typically craft. The popularity of Bart's creations has gradually grown. People from as far as Norway, Sweden, Japan and New York are in possession of a *Bartholomew Original.*

This sculpture was a disaster. His trembling caused the rod to rotate poorly. The glass folded in on itself, stopping short of total collapse. Yet, it was auctioned for a mind-boggling amount, as if the time lapse between pieces added to its worth. One art critique wrote: 'Bartholomew's latest work is the embodiment of grief.'

I am no longer certain if grief plays any part in Bart's moods, which sway between vicious anger and total apathy. It appears to be more of a habit. A habit he has no reason to break. We own the house outright. We inherited money from both sets of parents. His languid depression is a luxury most humans cannot afford. I've often wondered if I would better serve him by draining the bank accounts, giving the whole lot to charity. Perhaps then he would see reason to emerge.

The therapist tells me I misunderstand his disease. That it is a disease. A part of him is broken and should be respected as much as if he'd shattered his tibia, ruptured a spinal disc. Care should be administered, as surely as if he were bound to a hospital bed. Thus, each morning I am to approach my husband's side with profound gentleness. I am not to say, 'Just get up. There are things to do and people to see.' No, I am to say, 'You appear to be having a spot of trouble rising this morning. Is there anything I can do to assist?' This requires a plenitude of patience. And kindness. And fortitude. All of which I lack. Because what I would dearly love to do is to toss a bucket of cold water across this slumbering heap. Such an action, I suppose, would soak the mattress and could lead to mould. A great pity, indeed.

I suppress a sigh and leave. Stepping over a trail of ants, which are doubtlessly doing untold damage to our hardwood floors, I enter the en suite. The original home had no such frills. It is a renovation orchestrated by my mother-in-law after the death of her husband. Upon its completion, she phoned Bart, 'That Ms Spinner of yours will not be able to object to moving in now, the house boasts the latest amenities.'

She never did forgive me for keeping my own name.

'I am the last one,' I once said to her, 'and you must admit, there are still a plethora of Simonds about.'

She'd been aghast. 'Simonds, perhaps, but not *the* Simonds of the third cousin of the original Huguenots that…'

I have never been able to precisely trace her version of *the* Simond family tree, of which Bart is apparently the last. Nonetheless, I bore her a small olive branch in the form of Kai Simond, only to have her tear it loose.

The bathroom door shuts with a quiet click. Beneath my feet, the marble tiles are slick with chill. It's as if I've entered the cold tomb of an ancient Egyptian god. The entire design is at odds with the old sandstone home. It contains his and hers raised bowl sinks above granite countertops. It creates an eye-watering glare under the recessed lights, which were installed *sans* dimmer switch. The enormous shower is equipped with numerous jets, poised to lay siege on the body from all angles. Bart, in a rare moment of productivity, disabled the extras. Now the main showerhead uses solar-heated borehole water, which drains into a recycle tank for the toilets. His enthusiasm for the project had given me hope. A turning point, I'd believed then. But it had been nothing more than the eye of the storm.

There is no bathtub in the en suite. My Pretoria born and raised mother-in-law detested them. She could not swim. Until Bart was old enough to shower, the nanny was under strict instruction only to sponge bathe him. I may have felt some empathy for her phobia if the damn woman had been consistent. Instead, her hypocrisy was a fatal flaw.

Not that I would ever take a bath, should I have the choice.

Reaching out, I turn the taps. The shower emits a warm earth-scented spray. Stepping into it, a knot at the base of my neck begins to unclench. I tilt my face, enjoying the feel of the water running through my hair, slipping between my breasts, over my belly, streaming along the curves of my buttocks like a caress. There are so few of those these days.

A click announces the opening of the bathroom door. Bart stumbles in. For a moment I am pleased that he has managed to rise without assistance. But then, without even a 'hello,' he plops onto the toilet. A loud, distasteful noise echoes from the bowl, followed by the sound of solid matter hitting water. The room fills with the odour of his waste.

'There are other toilets free,' I say.

'I'm fine,' he says from lips that barely move.

I bite the inside of my cheek, the only thing I can do to keep from screaming, 'I'm not!'

The therapist says I have the right to express my needs. Boundaries can and should be drawn, even as I continue to reassure Bart, to be there for Bart, to routinely express willingness to help Bart. The therapist warns there is a danger between the depressed and the spouse developing a damaging co-dependent relationship.

'Sounds a lot like co-parenting, then,' I'd said.

The therapist was startled mute for a moment. I was pleased. The man is vile. He's an old family friend of my in-laws. 'Such a good man,' my mother-in-law would say each visit. Not that anything he said or did resulted in a single morsel crossing her lips, eventually leaving her too weak to fend off the common flu. But the man makes house calls, and my husband accepts his presence. 'It's nice of him to drop by,' Bart says, as if the therapist popped around for a cup of tea out of the goodness of his heart. The man drinks many cups of tea, which I am obliged to serve him. Then I pay him, in cash, from my own funds.

Bart flushes the toilet. For a moment, the smell intensifies. He pulls up his threadbare grey boxers, closes the lid and sits down upon it, forgoing washing his hands.

'Would you care to join me?'

He shakes his head. He never does. We've had sex exactly three times since the funeral. Each time Bart went soft before either of us climaxed. It has been precisely nine months since our last attempt.

'I need sex,' I told him once.

He grabbed my laptop, pulling up an adult toy website. 'Which ones would you like?'

'I need real sex,' I'd said. 'With a person.'

'So have an affair, if it is so damn important to you.'

'Would you really want that?'

'No, I wouldn't want that. What kind of fucked up husband do you think I am?'

'What? It was you who suggested –'

'We were talking about you. Your *need* to have sex. You, not understanding that I can't right now. You, unwilling to abstain while I grieve. You, wanting to whore around.'

Sobbing, I had fled to my garden.

He never apologised. A week later, however, a large unmarked box was delivered. It was full of an array of gadgets: vibrators, dildos, anal plugs and three varieties of lube. I was torn between wanting to toss it at his head and being in awe that he'd gone to such trouble. Even on his better days, the demand to punch in his credit card details overwhelms him and he gives up before checking out. When I'm feeling generous, I revisit the website and complete the purchase. Sometimes he is grateful. Other times he says, 'Waste of money.'

Whereupon I wish to reply, 'And you are a waste of life.'

I step to the side of the water and ring out my hair. Then I open the shower door, reaching for my towel. 'I've left it on for you.'

'I'm fine,' he says, watching as I cocoon my flesh in thick cotton.

'No, it is not fine, Bart,' I say, temper rising. 'You must shower. We are meeting the guys at the shop. Noon. Remember?'

'You are wasting water.'

'Then please, get in.'

I shoot him a pointed look. He cowers, a quivering dog who knows he has offended his master. Slowly he stands up and lets his boxers drop. They are so filthy I want to vomit. Instead, I reach down and pick them up. 'I'll put these in the laundry for you,' I say, tossing them into the basket tucked in the corner. His t-shirt follows, plopping at my feet. I lean over and nab it, pitching it into the same basket.

He remains where he is, naked, smelly. 'Go on,' I say.

He steps under the water, gingerly, like an elderly man. I pass over a face cloth and a bar of soap, imbedded with the essence of St. John's Wort. The herbalist who sold it to me was full of assurances that the flower could somehow breach the epidermis, inspiring my husband to seize the day. So far, the only effect I've discerned is that Bart smells significantly better after using it.

He stands there, water streaming behind him, face cloth in one hand, soap in the other. 'Go ahead,' I say, shutting the shower door.

'I do know how to wash myself,' he says, but does not move.

I wait.

The water keeps running, nicking his shoulder blades, narrowly missing his butt.

'I can climb back in, if that will help,' I say.

This, apparently, is such an appalling suggestion that he begins to rapidly apply soap to cloth, cloth to body, lathering from greasy head to scaly heel. It is difficult to not take insult. With a tight smile, I depart.

I dress with angry jerks, thrusting my legs through the jeans, snapping on my vest, yanking up the zip to the tracksuit top. Bart gave me the last item, a surfer brand, in better times. The crazy doodles chasing the geometric scatters are far too cheerful, despite the black background. But I need to cling to the good Bart. Today is daunting enough without forgetting the man he is capable of being.

I give the bathroom door a glance, weighing the pros and cons of popping my head in. He could require assistance in getting out. It has been necessary often enough. Or my nosey look-in may anger him, so that he stomps back to bed to remain there for the rest of the day. Both are equally possible. But the latter would mean forgoing the meeting at noon. He got out of bed without my help. This should be a sign that he'll manage. With that, I head to the kitchen to make a cup of tea. I predict this day will require many, many cups of tea.

Luxolo phoned me yesterday. He can phone only me. Nobody can call Bart. He smashed his cell phone the evening that everything changed. Then he obliterated our landlines. He left my cell. 'Isn't safe for you to go without.' Even in deep rage and grief there was a shred of rationale. So much for artistic temperament.

In time, I went out and bought a wireless internet device for my laptop. The laptop is routinely borrowed. Despite this, he cannot be bothered to check his email. Unless people drop in (they never do) there is no other way to contact my husband but through me. I have become the filter between my husband and the outside world.

'Ella,' Luxolo had said yesterday, 'we cannot go on like this. Bart must start working.'

'I will try. But if the issue is money, then don't give Bart his share. He doesn't deserve it.'

'Ella, the finances don't work like that. And that isn't the real issue, hey? We need hands. Hands that know what they are doing.'

'Have you considered training somebody?'

'There is no time to get anyone up and running before season. We need a working pair, now.'

'He'll cover the shortfall. Just write it down as if we purchased the missing stock.'

'Hey, listen. Please. It isn't just the bills. We don't want charity. We want a fully functioning workshop. I've got pride. And damn it, Jama and Dumisani have kids, hey? Not trying to be insensitive, but you know what I mean. They want to be somebody their kids can look up to. Get it?"

'Yes.' It came out in a whisper.

'Ah Ella, I'm sorry.'

My throat tightened. 'Don't.'

'I didn't mean – '

His voice was desperate. Pleading. But it wasn't the time to have that conversation. 'Don't.'

'Fine. We'll see you tomorrow.'

'Tomorrow?' A feeling, perhaps betrayal, fluttered through. Even now I can't believe he insisted upon it.

'Ella, we're all busy.'

'Yes, I know. But tomorrow I've already promised Kamala to take photographs and –'

'I am well aware of that and everything else. But Jama and Dumisani are ready to lose it.'

'Yes, of course. Sorry. Tomorrow, then,' I said, as if it were as good as done.

But tomorrow has now arrived, and Bart is not a tide table. I cannot promise this will happen, even if he has showered today. Old Bart is still absent. With even a fraction of the former man, it would be easy to make him understand how imperative it is that he comes to the workshop at noon. He loves these men and would never wish them harm. In each one Bart found a kindred spirit, an artist, and trained them to be masters of glass. His three employees, pseudo-partners, are now his brothers of both fire and sea. Luxolo is the scuba diver, Jama and Dumisani prefer the sturdiness of the boogie board. But they all are able to surf well enough. Occasionally Bart would be amenable to boogie board, but he never dives.

'Suffocating,' he has said.

I find this baffling. At least with diving a person has an oxygen tank. There is no such assistance when a surfer performs a duck dive, holding his breath as the waves roll past.

'You wouldn't understand,' Bart said. 'You'd have to be willing to swim with your head wet to even have a chance of getting it.'

He couldn't make such a statement now. Well, he could. But he would be wrong. Which only shows how far we have drifted from one other's reality.

Blowing gently on my tea, I walk out onto the stoep. It faces directly north, welcoming the sun. The mountaintops have lost their purple tones and are now glaringly green. Free of clouds and mist, I can make out the outcrops and crevices with sharp clarity.

I cannot, however, see the ocean beneath. It is the only northern beach in all of South Africa. Given my in-laws' resources, they could have easily afforded prime beachside property. But my mother-in-law was adamant that she would not live in a home with a sea view.

She was convinced a tsunami would someday wash away Mossel Bay: 'I have no desire to see the end coming.'

Such a person is not typically suited to living on a peninsula. But her real estate tycoon of a husband's idea of middle ground was buying a large, double plot property high up on the hill. It is set so far back that the bay is obscured. Only the mountains are visible, giving the illusion that there is land at their base. Oudtshoorn would have probably been a much fairer compromise.

Then Bart became a surfer. They say all children rebel.

*

Once upon a time, my mother-in-law kept two Shetland ponies on the property's second plot. They were her beloveds, who were immortalised in her home's interior décor. To this day, I am tossing out the countless knick-knacks that littered the house.

From all accounts, the ponies were useless creatures. They were so small only a toddler could have ridden them, should my mother-in-law have allowed such a thing. She did not. Nor did she breed them. They could not provide the family with milk or eggs. They hardly made a house-worthy companion, like a dog or a cat, despite their devotion. Yet, proudly she strolled them through the streets for their daily exercise. The town adored her for it. To this day, many local establishments display photographs of the three of them parading down the main thoroughfares.

When the ponies passed on, my father-in-law considered selling the extra land. 'Then we'll have neighbours spying on us,' my mother-in-law said. Her words gave him pause, and he was still weighing the value of currency versus privacy on the day he dropped dead of a heart attack.

'If you move in,' my mother-in-law told Bart, 'then I won't have to sell the plot. Your Ms Spinner can hardly object, she'll finally be able to upgrade her hobby from window boxes to a proper garden.'

It was the land – not the en suite bathroom with its array of jets – that had me agreeing to dwell in in-law purgatory. I craved the great space, empty but for the old coach shed in the far south-east corner, now converted into a granny flat. The lush, well-fertilised soil is a gardener's paradise.

Perhaps the whole thing is entirely my fault, after all.

No, I will not do this. Scooping up two wicker baskets, I make my way to the land that is now my garden. As I pass by the chicken tractor, I give it its daily shove. The birds squawk their protest, despite their delight in the virgin soil now beneath them, waiting to be scratched. Then with a critical eye, I survey the carefully arranged raised beds and examine the offerings. At last there is asparagus ready to be clipped. I am not often generous with it. But today seems to require a sacrifice of sorts. Something to appease whatever in the universe can be appeased. I need a good day. I wonder what the therapist would say to that?

The baskets gradually fill: strawberries, a few artichokes, bunches of rosemary, oregano and mint.

Baskets full, I bring them to the stoep. My trays of chard wave to me. 'Plant us today,' they say. I really should be going. My friends are waiting. But Ecclesiastes says, 'Sow your seeds in the morning,' and I firmly believe this also holds true with plants.

Grabbing an old bucket, I go around the corner and add compost. Then I return to the stoep. With a glance through the window to confirm Bart is nowhere near, I quietly slip inside. On the mantel sits a glass box, shifting with the colours of the calm before the storm. Gently, the lid is raised. A teaspoon of the contents is measured out and added to the bucket. Lid replaced, I return to the garden, only then daring to breathe. I mix the earth with water, compost and the stolen touch of Kai's ashes, creating a rich soil that will help the chard thrive. 'May you travel far and wide,' I whisper, as I plant the first few.

A number of cucumbers of decent size distract me from my task. I promptly gather the bloated green phalluses, which have intrigued since discovering they are up to ninety-five percent water.

Back on the stoep, I rearrange the contents with care. My friend Kamala insists that presentation matters in the offering of quaint organic foods. Apparently, people want to experience in its entirety the goodness that organic represents. This, according to Kamala, includes wicker baskets. Wicker baskets are goodness. Perhaps I should have allowed Kai to slumber in one rather than share our bed at night and take his naps in a standard cot. Tradition says that Moses once slept in basket, hiding in the reeds, and God favoured him. After all, Moses was allowed to reach adulthood.

Heading back towards the chard, I notice the coriander. It never lasts long in this climate. But for now, it is a grand display of generosity. I rush over and clip huge swaths. This herb gives Kamala such pleasure. Every time she is presented with some, she immerses her face in the soft fragrant leaves, inhaling deeply. The afterglow from her coriander encounters has me convinced she is a passionate lover.

Tourists are always surprised that Kamala is part-owner of the café, since its name, Plato's Bru, has a distinctly Grecian slant that reflects her husband's heritage.

'Do you serve curry?' the tourists always ask.

'The art doesn't automatically pass down the gene pool, eh?' she always replies.

Kamala does make curry. Thick, gorgeous creations that always have me eating well past the point of fullness. But she only makes these dishes for those she loves. 'Why ruin something wonderful by turning it into a business?' she says.

In the distance the gate bell rings. I ignore it as I gently place the coriander into the baskets. The bell rings again. I want to call out to Bart, 'Answer the bloody intercom; I'm busy,' but don't. There is no point. Answering the gate is a task that no longer concerns him, along with using a cell phone or email, or paying bills or making love to his wife. Like work, though perhaps today that will change.

The gate bell rings a third time as I rise from my knees. 'I'm coming,' I say, despite the fact that only the passing butterfly has heard. I take the more leisurely route, rounding the house, rather than passing through it, hoping the extra time will encourage whoever it is to give up and depart. But as I'm about to clear the corner, the bell lets out another ring.

A few more steps and I can see the source of this morning's noise. 'Good morning,' he says, in an accent that sounds vaguely familiar, yet is most certainly not South African.

I nod, stopping my step just short of the gate.

He is a tall, well-built man, of impressive stature. But his skin is as foreign as his accent: dark, like a La Rochelle grape, giving off a bluish tinge. I suppose he is a wanderer, from some-where-else in the great African beyond. Although his state of dress suggests a British second-hand shop: heavyweight tweed trousers, a cotton button down and a flat cap. All are excellent quality, but greatly worn.

'My name is Dylan, ma'am. I have been told you have need of a gardener.'

My mind whirls, trying to comprehend what is happening. What has already happened. People have discussed me, my garden, possibly even my husband. I am aware, of course, that this is a small town and people talk. That Bart and I are spoken about among others. But to have this irrefutable proof of gossip at my gate is an entirely different matter. This is vast. This is personal.

I tilt my head, waiting for Dylan to say more. A name of who sent him? After all, I have never expressed a desire to hire a gardener. My guess is Luxolo. He worries, claiming I'm doing too much. If Kamala or Thad had thought I required a gardener, then Kamala would have said so. Not a woman to mince her words. Jama and Dumisani would never dream of doing something so bold. They mind their own business. If something needs to be said, they leave it to Luxolo to say it. There is nobody else in the town that would try to assist; their gossip is to fill time, not to reach solutions.

The man remains silent. Perfectly still, posture military straight. I have not witnessed a person carry himself in such a manner in a long time. His eyes are taking me in, surveying the front of our property. What he concludes about us, however, is indiscernible.

I lick my lips, suddenly self-conscious of their dry, cracked state.

His eyes flicker to me.

Maybe Kamala is right; I should start using balm. She claims that I am neglecting myself. But for whom should I now prepare myself? A man looking for work?

I tilt my head to the other side.

No movement. Yet, there is no air of impatience, nor does he appear to be trying to use his physique to intimidate. This is important. I could not bear to have an overly active sort bouncing along my property requiring constant approval. Nor could I tolerate a man who feels he can bully me into offering work. It is different, this quality Dylan possesses, from the usual stranger who rings my gate. Dignity. That must be what this is, this unwavering silence. So I suppose he will not beg or plead, but feels he has said enough. Fair enough. Now do I have need for a gardener or not?

'Where do you live?' I say.

'Best not to ask, ma'am.'

I almost insist he answer, but stop the words from rushing out. Do I really want to know? Do I desire another worry to dwell on at 2am, haunting the shadows, so I can spill tears for yet another soul or place that never asked for my prayers? Perhaps he is correct. It is best to leave it.

Still he waits. No apology for dodging my question. Still feels worthy of work.

Dignity. What an amazing attribute to have. I am not certain Bart has any, and I greatly question if I have ever possessed such self-worth.

'Fine, then,' I say.

'To what, ma'am?'

All of it, I think. To not knowing where you live, to not knowing where you come from, to not pressing if Dylan is really your name, to having you employed.

I push the button and the gate begins to roll back. He takes two long steps across the track.

'You are welcome to begin today, if that suits.' This hardly seems necessary. He is here, on my property, waiting and ready. He will work. 'Of course, if the arrangement proves satisfactory to us both then you will have to come on Mondays and Thursdays. Those are the days Happiness comes to clean. It would be best, you see.'

He nods.

A sunbird flies past, and my gaze follows it. The bird lands on the hydrangea. I loathe its bloated blooms, but it was one of my mother-in-law's most cherished shrubs. To uproot it would be misinterpreted, perceived as an attack on her memory. So the hydrangea stays until my husband is well enough to understand that this is not about his mother, I simply despise the plant.

'Is Happiness happy?' he asks.

The question catches me off guard and rattles inside my skull. There is no simple explanation for Happiness. She is a woman who sings softly while tending to her tasks. She counts every blessing, continuously lifting praise to God. She is punctual, practical and thorough with her work. Over the years I have watched her belly expand five fruitless times. A few months back she came to work and said, 'He made a baby with someone else.' I put the kettle on and spooned three sugars into her favourite mug. We sat in silence while she took shaky sips. She has not spoken of the incident since.

I say to Dylan, 'Happiness is highly devoted to the Lord.'

The corners of his mouth turn upward into a wry grin. It is the first time his face has lost the perfectly smooth look of expressionless composure. 'Aren't we all, ma'am.'

No, I think. But since I have avoided his question, the least I can do is grant him the last word.

*

I'm at a loss at what to do with Dylan. I must go. But he is now here. I cannot have someone blundering through my plants when I've yet to establish if he knows the difference between a dandelion and a gooseberry vine.

As we walk, me pointing out this and that, Dylan's eyes calmly roam the property. He studies the house and its surrounding grounds with great care. 'Ma'am, have you been tending all this yourself?'

A lie sits at the tip of my tongue, but before I release it Bart stumbles out onto the back stoep. He looks drugged. He wobbles onto the overgrown lawn; his legs are weak. My husband has always had a slim build, but these days he is scrawny, muscle wasting away, and with it his sense of balance. I doubt he could surf even if he found the desire.

My feet have stopped moving and so have Dylan's. I should have a witty phrase to smooth over this awkward moment. But the words fail to materialise. It seems I no longer possess the energy or the inclination to excuse my husband's actions. Bart is who he now is. So together, Dylan and I stare as Bart gives a final flop into the hammock strung up between an avo and a mango tree. The trees' placement, along the right side of the formal garden, provides a buffer to the side road. They are the only things my mother-in-law ever put into the earth that truly pleases me.

Dylan says nothing. I suppose there is not much one can say.

Bart lets out a long sigh. It is so full of despondence that I can practically see a dark grey cloud rising to hover above him.

I should lead Dylan somewhere. Show him something. Move away from this scene.

The hammock releases an audible fart.

I wince.

'Gardening is a passion to which we are not all called,' Dylan says. He has said the perfect words. I cannot bear any more sympathy, yet I am too raw for jokes or scorn. But there is something very wrong with ignoring the decay of a person's humanity. Dylan has seen Bart, acknowledged Bart, without forcing me to discuss Bart.

I feel one of the marbles lodged in my gut begin to dissolve, releasing my feet from their invisible bind. I begin to lead Dylan across the overgrown lawn towards the garden shed. Perhaps this gardener will be more than a burden gained from my inability to say no. Perhaps Dylan is a good addition to our lives. Good, like a wicker basket.

Stopping at the door to the shed, I offer a small smile. 'I'm afraid I have no passion for mowing the lawn.'

'That is completely understandable, ma'am. Shall I begin with that?'

'Yes,' I say. 'And it's Ella.'

'Of course, ma'am.'

It has been over two months since I last made use of the lawnmower. The machine had repeatedly cut out, driving me to fury. Peering into the shed, I squint into the dim light, trying to locate the blasted thing. It is Dylan who eventually extends a finger, pointing to a wheel poking out from the tangle of rakes, shovels and a frightfully long extension cord. Together we wrestle it out. Before I can apologise for its shoddy state, he drops to one knee. After examining it in great detail, he gives a firm nod. 'I can work this, ma'am.'

I show him where the grass clipping should go. He runs his eyes over the compost bin. 'You could use another of these, ma'am.'

'It's Ella, and yes, well, I'm sure in time I'll sort it out eventually.'

'If you wish, I could build you one, ma'am.'

'Ella. And yes, that could be good. Perhaps we discuss this later? I'm running a bit late.'

Even as the words leave my mouth I know how ridiculous I sound. A childless woman, no longer formally employed, is never late. Wherever could she possibly need to be? To get her nails done? Her hair? I want to laugh, but know if I begin I won't stop.

Dylan, however, is taking no notice. He is adjusting bits of the lawnmower with deliberate intent. He looks up. 'Perhaps if I finish this before you return, I could trim back some of the bushes around the house?'

'That sounds like a good plan,' I say, knowing full well it needs it. Unable to rip out my mother-in-law's landscaping and unable to muster the energy to care for her tastes, I've allowed it to rot into a gardener's version of Ms Havisham's wedding dress.

Turning to go into the house, I spot the remaining chard, still waiting to be planted. I rush over, kneeling down beside their wee leaves with red and yellow stems. Footsteps come up behind me. 'Ma'am, I would be happy to do that as well, if you wish.'

I glance over my shoulder. 'No, I'm fine. Thank you, but no. It will only take me a moment.'

His expression is unreadable, but I am sure I must sound barking mad. How to explain? I can't. As the headmistress at my boarding school used to say, 'Discretion is a virtue too often overlooked.' I say nothing. Thankfully he does not press the point and, without further comment, returns to the lawnmower.

The moment leaves me exhausted, sad. A desire to quit beckons. My eyes sting, willing me to give in. Pressing my teeth firmly down on my tongue I mentally begin stacking the bricks, focusing on this day's plans: Kamala this morning, the meeting at noon, Luxolo at three. I repeat the mantra over and over again, stacking the bricks higher. My heartbeat slows. A deep breath and then another. At last the final chard is planted without incident. Each one receives a gentle pat with the edge of my fingertips before I dash indoors.

For a moment the location of my camera eludes me. It has been so long. There was a time when it lived around my neck. I wanted to hold every moment. Show everyone how the world looks through my eyes. Beauty was everywhere, even in the wrinkle of flesh or a can abandoned in the gutter. I wanted to treasure all of it as the lens pulled me through each day, providing a way to interact with South Africa.

Returning to South Africa was an assault on the senses. I had spent so many years in England, first in boarding school and then university. It was like being thrown a surprise party by hundreds upon hundreds of people who all rushed to greet me at once while a band played, obscuring the voices. Cape Town has so much sun, so much wind, so many conversations, so much hooting, so much poverty, so much garish display of wealth. It is vast, yet congested; I could spread my arms and twirl without hitting anyone, then the next moment be crushed.

It was the camera that held the onslaught at bay so that I could tease out the individuals. The camera made sense of the crisscross patterns between motorist and pedestrian on the city streets. The camera gave me a reason to say hello. But since Kai died, my life has been frozen. A single, still image.

Today, however, demands my rather out-of-date photographic machine. I should have done this last night when I unearthed the battery pack from my desk. What if it no longer works? Kamala will be so disappointed. She may think I've done this on purpose.

A memory tugs, blooming into frame. It is so clear and perfect there is no need to search. Of course I put it there.

Gently I open the door, peeping in like a mother checking on her slumbering baby. There is no one waiting for me on the other side. This is now the guest room for the visitors who have never arrived. The walls remain the same pale yellow with green trim. But the curtains with the surfboard print are long gone, replaced with drapes in striped panels of greens and pinks. On the plain pine double bed is a white duvet with dark green vines that bear gold flowers, tinged with pinks. The three little pine shelves on the windowless wall still hold a wooden airplane and three antique tin cars. Gone is the general debris that comes with childrearing. That has been swept away to decompose far from here.

I open the wardrobe, taking care not to glance down. I know they remain. I cannot forget. The series of tiny handprints running along the door's bottom border is imprinted on my brain. Each one is dated, the last when Kai turned eighteen-months. I was waiting for his second birthday to do the next set. I worried that if done too often, we would run out of space.

Sucking in my gut, I reach up and grasp the camera case.

'What are you doing?'

I spin around, as if I've been caught making mischief. There is Bart, wobbly, but alert. It seems unfathomable that he devoted so much energy to seek me out. My mouth fills with words, too many words, making it impossible to enunciate a single syllable.

He steps forward and slowly reaches behind me. The wardrobe door swings shut with a hush. His hands place themselves around mine, which are cupping the camera. His hands are soft. When did they shed their callused protection?

'Are you working today?' he asks.

'A wedding,' I say, so fast the lie leaves a breeze in its wake.

He nods in a careful, considered manner. 'Friday…an unusual day to get married.'

I swallow as my heart bears down with such strength that my abdominal muscles weep. He knows the day of the week. The same man who said, 'Who gives a flying fuck?' the last time I told him the date. But today he has decided that it matters. He knows it is Friday. All on his own. This is significant. My fingers spasm in reflex, but my poor camera cannot capture this moment in any tangible sense.

His hands give mine a squeeze as his lips brush against my forehead. My eyes shut and my breath ceases, as if exhaling would blow him into the hallway, shatter his bones.

'Enjoy,' he says, stepping back.

I open my eyes. 'Thanks.'

He turns, unsteadily, to leave.

'Um, and I'll see you a bit later?' I say, trying to keep the desperate edge from my voice. 'Thought we'd leave at 11:45?'

He shrugs. 'Maybe.' Then his fragile limbs propel him forward, head carefully balanced in the manner of a child first learning to walk.

My stomach hurts.

Perhaps I should stay.

No. The camera is operable. The wicker baskets are brimming. Dylan is outside. Bart wouldn't. Not with someone here.

He'll be fine.

The air of the Prius is tepid, like a long-standing cup of tea whose tannin clings to the taste buds, leaving the mouth craving a fresh drink. The day is already fading into the shadows of the what-could-have-beens. It is unwise to overanalyse Bart's behaviour in the guestroom – the kiss on the forehead, his hands touching mine. We have been here before, only to fall back time, time, again. But it is difficult to resist. I want to sit down with a cuppa and contemplate.

Tea is a soul-deep comforting drink. It's making is an act of reincarnation. First, a seedling is placed into the dampened earth. After three years of careful tending – watering, fertilising, protecting from wind and insects and other ills – the leaves are harvested after the first flush. Then they are processed to extract that carefully maintained water. When stored, it is imperative that moisture is kept out. Yet to drink, water is again added.

But when I reach the café Thad will serve coffee, which is tough and brawny. This is probably why the Greek is so fond of it. To him, coffee is second only to ouzo. Unfortunately, Kamala can't stand the aperitif. This is scandalous to Thad's family. As he put it, 'If my papa had not already passed, he'd have had to die all over again.'

Kamala remains unrepentant.

A small bend in the road brings the view to its full glory. The mountains remain clear and I can now see individual homes across the bay. So much water. It seems unfathomable that Mossel Bay, surrounded by an abundance of liquid blue, is prone to drought. Yet, that is the paradox this town often faces.

Water is not good like a wicker basket.

A red light brings me to a halt. People begin crossing the street, in front of me, behind me. One man almost careens into my passenger side, but catches himself, his elbow brushing the side mirror. Relief courses through me. What would I have done had he fallen? Helped? Driven on?

The light turns green. I turn right on to Marsh Street, the town's main road. Despite the early hour, there are already cars parking beside the pavement. People open their doors without looking, dashing into the shop for a newspaper, hustling off to check their post. These swinging doors create an obstacle course for the taxis, cyclists, pedestrians and other vehicles. It is like joining a freeform dance, as we weave in and out of each other's lanes. Open, shut, open, shut – there is no warning. It is a moment. The door is either missed, or hit. For another car it is a scratch, a dent, a broken headlight. For a cyclist it can mean the end of life.

Time is vast. It is the individual moments that kill.

I stop at the crossing. A 4x4 drives by, coasting down the hill towards the sea. I pull off, passing the defunct Milkwood Cottage Cuisine on the corner. I cannot look at the place without recalling the flying pieces of Bart's cell phone. I feel satisfaction tinged with shame at the For Sale sign still standing forlorn in the increasingly dingy window. They closed mere months after Kai passed. If I were a fair and kind person, I would bear them no ill will. They had nothing to do with Kai's fate. But I cannot muster compassion for a man who gave Bart so little.

'Please sir, let's step outside. . . I'm sorry, but you're disturbing the other guests.'

*

Kamala is on the stoep waiting for me. She is one of the rare and chosen few who looks regal and elegant no matter what she is doing or how she is dressed. Today is jeans and jewel-toned purple scoop neck, topped with a green corduroy coat and a flowing scarf.

'Thaddeus!' she calls over her shoulder. 'Ella is here. Get cooking.'

She practically glides down the four stone steps to the pavement, despite the hiking boots, despite the swollen belly. I am engulfed in a hug, her hard stomach pressing mine. She kisses both my cheeks. 'I was getting worried. Thought maybe it was too much.'

I step back and offer an apologetic smile. 'No, sorry, I am merely late. Delayed by the unexpected arrival of a gardener.'

'You hired a gardener?'

'It appears to be so.'

'I'm so happy!' She embraces me again. Her hugs are always tight, hard, all- consuming. They transfer a bit of the warmth and energy she exudes. I tolerate such affection from Kamala and only Kamala. Most people's hugs are suffocating; diminishing the receiver. They always want something and, like a leech, try to suck it out with their embrace. 'Help me,' their hugs seem to say.

But today, even her hug is too much. I carefully pull away, trying not to raise questions. It would be too difficult to explain. I do not want to leave the impression that I cannot bear my friends' impending parenthood, which is far from the case. Thad and Kamala are having their own baby. That baby will not be my son. Even if Bart and I, in another life, were to have a second baby, he or she would not be Kai. But Kamala has reached the stage of her pregnancy where others can feel the baby kick. Perhaps it would be fine if I felt the movement with my hand. But if it kicked against my own womb, I would retch.

'You didn't send the gardener, did you?' I say.

'No, but I wish I had. What a brilliant idea. Now come, you must tell me more.'

She tugs on my sleeve. I stop her with a motion to the boot of the car.

'Thaddeus,' she says over her shoulder, then she turns to reach into the boot, scooping out a handful of coriander. 'Ooooh, bless you. This is why you are my best friend.'

I pull out the camera.

She presses the soft fragrant leaves to her face. Her entire body transforms with delight.

Click.

'Hey, we are not starting that yet.' A slight tint stains her cheeks. She is beautiful.

Click.

'Ella!' She drops the coriander into the basket.

I shrug, lowering the camera. But I'm not the least bit sorry. If I had my way I'd photograph Kamala exclusively in a coriander patch while the wind ruffles her hair. Or I'd pile the herb high, creating a bed for her to lie on. She'd look exquisite, sensual. The difficulty would be keeping the coriander from wilting under the lights. The old me would have relished such a challenge and suggest we try. Ella of Now keeps quiet.

Thad comes jogging down the steps. He is wearing a t-shirt, baggy shorts and slops, the uniform of the typical laid-back surfer. Very Mossel Bay. 'Morning,' he says. A kiss on my cheek, a gentle hand on my back.

'Ah, cucumbers,' he says, as he lifts the baskets. When he walks off with the bounty, I can hear him telling the green phalluses how he will make tzatziki out of them. Thad once told me that as long as he can have his Greek food then he does not need Greece.

'But don't you miss your homeland?' I had asked.

'Have you seen the news about my country?' he'd said. 'Plato weeps!'

Kamala and I go inside to sit amongst the bric-a-brac. The café is stuffed with curious things to admire and fiddle with, including a host of used books. The homey atmosphere welcomes people in, while Kamala and Thad's warm personalities encourage conversation. But the organised clutter – a tossed quilt here, a stack of old iron weights there, a gaudy chandelier overhead – also allows the lone patron to be small, to slip behind an old cello and sip coffee in respite.

'Why do you think the Greeks were so wise?' Thad once said. 'Because they valued the space both to gather and to think.'

Kamala picks up my camera and examines it carefully before setting it back down. She looks me in the eye. 'Now tell me again, this gardener. What is he like?'

'Contemplative.'

'Slow?'

'His manner suggests he'll be thorough in his work. But he

chooses his words well. There is little waste in his speech.'

She grins. 'Then he's a good match for you. I, on the other hand, am not. May I tell you about my morning? Well too bad, because I'm going to.' With that, she launches into a colourful diatribe about an unsavoury customer.

Thad comes out and plonks down two steaming cups of Greek coffee, made on the stove, along with two glasses of water. I once asked for milk. It was a mistake.

'Kamala,' he says. 'You are not boring her with bacon-man, are you?'

'Yes I am.' She turns to me. 'What kind of imbecile demands an English fry up from a Greek restaurant, eh? I'm Indian, he is lucky we serve any meat.'

'In my country,' he says, 'there are people who think lamb is vegetarian.'

I put my hand on his. 'Thad, I've seen *My Big Fat Greek Wedding*, get over it. Besides, you also serve fish.'

'Oh no, now that is not meat,' he says. 'Fish is a fish, even the Catholics are allowed to eat it on Fridays.'

Kamala shakes her head. 'It is a living creature.'

'Not after you eat it,' he says.

The conversation keeps bouncing along, as if I am caught in the middle of a friendly table tennis match. It is both amusing and grating. I need their company, I know. If I allow myself to retreat any further, I will be sucked into the same vortex that grips Bart. Perhaps he is braver than I, or at least more honest. To act normal, to co-habit with the everyday routines of others takes monumental effort. And for what? So I can sit, aching, in the presence of comfortable, humorous marital dialogue.

It is not jealousy. This is much worse; it is nostalgia. With the former, a person can still hope to obtain the object of their desire. With the latter, one's time has passed. I know what these two have, because Bart and I used to have our own version of it. We had off the wall debates and inside jokes. Old Bart, upon hearing about bacon-man, would have given me a wink: 'Dude's not plaster-worthy.'

Plaster-worthy: that was our phrase. It isn't funny, or clever, but ours all the same. It was something that we shared between us that allowed a moment to be stretched, the first memory of us, and carry it alongside our growing lives.

I met Bart as he was emerging from the sea, surfboard under one arm. He was bleeding from a gash on his forehead. 'Would you like a plaster?' I had said, removing one from my shorts' pocket.

He'd given me a grin, managing to look handsome despite the blood marring his face. 'Ah, I see you are a sensible woman, always prepared. But I must ask, am I worthy of such a treasure?'

'Why not?' I'd laughed, pulling the prize slightly back. 'Or are there deep sins to confess?'

'Oh, we all have our sins. But I'd like to believe I'm plaster-worthy,' he'd said, plucking it from my fingertips.

I'm no longer certain my husband is plaster-worthy. I may well have been the type of woman to carry a plaster in her pocket, but I've always expected the recipient to reach out and apply the plaster himself. Now I live in constant resentment that a full-grown man requires me to hand him a bar of soap in order to wash.

As Kamala says to me, again and again, 'When are you going to start taking care of you?'

Tomorrow, I always think. Maybe that's Bart's answer too. Or perhaps that is far too optimistic.

The marital chatter ceases when Thad wanders off to help a customer. Kamala toys with her cup, studying me closely. I sip my coffee, trying to pull off an air of normalcy.

'Let's have it,' she says. 'What has your man done today?'

'Nothing,' I say.

'There's a surprise,' she says, shaking her head. 'You want me to go there and yank him out of bed?'

I give up trying to act like a normal person and allow my shoulders to hunch. 'No. He showered. He …' I take a few breaths. Kamala waits. For all her bubbling exuberance, she does listen. She is capable of patient quiet. I begin again, choosing my words with care, about this morning, about Luxolo's phone call, about my fear that Bart will not make the meeting at noon.

She sets down her coffee with purpose. 'Luxolo is an ass.'

I shrug.

'Exactly,' she says, throwing her arms out. 'You see my point. I mean, what's that man doing asking you, who's got enough on her own plate, to go help him out? If he wants Bart to show up and hold newspapers or whatever the hell they think he is strong enough to do, then they can pick Bart's sorry butt up.'

Guilt tugs at my conscience, pointing out everything Luxolo has done for me. 'I don't think it's like that, exactly. I mean he does …' Then again, it was he that insisted on having the meeting today. Despite the fact that he knew I was going to be dusting off the camera for the first time in over a year. Despite –

'Bullshit!' Kamala exclaims.

A customer turns around to stare.

'I'm sorry,' she says. 'No, actually I'm not. This whole damn town has left you – you! – to tend to Bart. We, his friends, need to start taking a more active role. They do interventions for drug users and anorexics. There must be something for people like Bart.'

'It's fine. Please.' I hunch forward, tighter, around the marble hardening in my gut.

'No, it isn't. But I'm going to call Luxolo. We're going to make a plan.'

Thad returns bearing two platters full of croissants and fresh fruit. A handful of my strawberries have lost their tiny green hats. Their blood red juice gleams from the beheading, begging to be licked.

Thad gives his wife a kiss on the lips. 'I could hear you in the kitchen.'

'Good,' she says. 'Then I don't have to tell you about it later.'

He shakes his head, before planting a kiss on the top of mine. 'She's a bully. Tell my wife to treat you nice.'

I smile.

She flicks a strawberry at him.

'Hey,' I say. 'I grew that.'

Thad picks it up off the floor and pops it in his mouth. The customer is staring again. He smiles at her. 'I believe in standing by my claim that this place is so clean you could eat off of the floor.' Whistling, he strides away.

Kamala laughs. Thankfully, so does the customer. The new marble slows its expansion. Kamala looks at me expectantly.

I glance down at the platter, with the lickable strawberries and tempting pastry. I pick up the croissant and hold it under her nose. 'Are these Greek or Indian?'

'They are damn delicious, and you'll eat 'em if you're smart.'

It's like biting into a flavourful air pocket. Flakes scatter across my plate as my tongue rolls the slightly sweet warmth around my mouth. 'Mmm,' I say.

'They better be, I spent ages figuring out how to make the perfect pre-made croissant so all Thad has to do is pop them in the oven.'

She sticks her knife into a tiny pot of butter – real butter, purchased from a local organic dairy – and carefully transfers it to her croissant with patient short strokes. 'People rarely understand the art of spreading old fashioned butter,' she says. 'It requires preparation, remembering to remove it from the fridge a half hour before use. Now people spend time as if there will always be more.'

Like the handprints, I think.

Her knife pauses mid-air as she studies her work. This is not an act simply to sweep our earlier words from our table. Kamala is a person who loves large, but these seemingly small things also truly interest her. She would have been well suited for the philosophy course she'd dreamt of. But her parents would only pay for further education if she attended the college of accounting. 'Practical people,' Kamala says. 'They saw how much their own accountant was costing them and decided to create their own.'

My parents insisted I study economics. 'You'll have to manage your trust someday,' they said. Scant weeks after graduation, I inherited everything. Faulty old gas heater combined with brand new double-glazing that sealed tight-tight made for a deadly combination. They say that it is a peaceful way to die. I may have been the only mother in our baby group who had installed a carbon monoxide detector. Overprotective and paranoid, they'd teased. Yet their bouncy bundles of joy still live, all of them. I sometimes wonder, with all the tragedy, if we are paying the price for some ancient family sin.

Perhaps I should have studied theology.

Instead, all I have offered the universe today is spring's first asparagus.

'I will trade you exactly one strawberry for your thoughts,' Kamala says.

There are some things best left unconfessed. Dwelling on death is one of them.

'Ella?'

'Coriander.'

'I'm intrigued. Tell me more.' She folds her hands under her chin, looking adorable and attentive without a bit of saccharine.

I clear my throat; no idea what I will say. But a piece of Ella-from-before rises and seizes my vocal cords. I seem to float above the table, watching this curious conversation between my best friend and my old self. The two women look happy, animated, like people who have actual lives that give them something worth saying.

It is true; once-upon-a-time Ella had a legitimate life. In addition to her arty pics, she made a day job out of being *the* edgy maternity photographer in town. She had mothers-to-be astride their Harleys, doing Spanish dancing, fishing, and arguing in court. 'Motherhood in action,' she called them. Women told her they wanted their babies to grow up and understand that mama had a life before nappies. She tried to keep the sentimental clichés at bay. Little time was spent positioning hands over the belly in the shape of a heart. Of course, time and time again, despite Ella's reputation, despite the praise, it was the heart that consistently sold. But the business made money – earned money – and that had felt good.

The spell breaks, and suddenly it is only me, Ella-of-today, sitting in the chair.

Kamala takes no notice, her eyes filled with wicked delight. 'That is a brilliant idea. We will do it.'

'But, I don't have –'

'No, not now. Relax. I'm not letting you get out of your promise. But we will do this shoot. Next year. You will plant that stuff in spades and I will proudly strut my post-partum body in front of your lens. I never know what to get Thad for Christmas, you see. I like to do something for his holiday, but he has so few needs.'

I nod. My husband has only one true need. Unfortunately, it is something he alone can give to himself. Forgiveness.

'You owe me a strawberry,' I say.

*

The engine of the Volvo rips into the silence, startling me. Thad turns from the wheel and reaches into the back seat to pat my knee. 'There, there, Ella, did the sound of my big bad petrol guzzling machine scare you?'

'Be nice,' Kamala says, from the passenger seat.

'I am always nice to Ella,' Thad says, and revs the engine.

I say nothing while pedestrians turn to look. Thad and Kamala wave. The pedestrians wave back. Mossel Bay is the kind of town where people acknowledge each other. Some claim it is because the locals are incredibly friendly. But I know that after the hearty acknowledgements, the whispers begin.

'Oh, you know her; it was her boy that drowned in the bathtub,' one will say. 'Ag, what a tragedy.'

'Oh yes, I do know about that. Ag, shame,' the other will say. 'Now her husband won't get out of bed. What a good son Bartholomew was. Bless.'

'Yes, yes. Shame. Really, really is. And his mother blamed herself. She died not long after. How I miss her and those ponies.'

'Oh, those ponies. They were an utter delight. A pity the daughter-in-law hasn't got some of her own. You'd think they'd give her a bit of comfort.'

'Ag, well you know how the young are. They always have to be different.'

It is the hint of British accent that makes people forget that I am perfectly capable of understanding Afrikaans.

'Are you okay?' Kamala asks, as Thad pulls away from the kerb.

'Yes,' I say.

She glances across the road, at the corner, where Milkwood Cottage Cuisine sits. 'Did you hear the owner finally died?'

I swallow carefully. 'No, I had not.'

Thad nods, glancing into the rearview mirror. 'Yeah, one of his kids phoned to see if we would be interested in the place. They've lowered the price.'

I shudder.

Thad nods. 'That about sums up my thoughts.'

Kamala tries to twist around in her seat, and fails abysmally. She sighs. 'Some day, Ella, Bart is going to quit blaming himself.'

I pick at my cuticle. 'I don't think either one of us will ever go back, even if somebody turned it into a completely different kind of establishment.'

'Fair enough,' Thad says, as we stop at the next corner. Stumbling by is a woman who often watches cars in front of the post office. She's lost her shoes and her head has been crudely shaved. She reaches the other side of the road with a jerk, then plods down the pavement.

'You girls sure did pick the perfect weather for this,' he says, rolling down the widow.

Inwardly, I groan. Speaking of the weather is the universal sign for awkwardness when conversing. Although I have yet to understand what it is people are left to discuss, now that politics and religion are considered crass. Mummy and baby group was a painful lesson in polite small talk, which required an air of grace I sadly lack. We prattled on about nappies and sleep habits *ad nauseam*. The few women brave enough (or foolhardy enough) to openly express opinions on any real matter of social weight left me wishing they had not. I almost liked you, I would think.

I envied Bart and his surfing. It gave him something he could discuss with others, no matter where he was. Even if people were not surfers, they would have questions about the sport. Or bring up sharks. The fearsome dorsal fin inspires many tales and gobbles up time.

Conversation fills time these days, nothing more. Maybe that is why people gossip in such quantities. Since Kai died I've often considered that it would be best if we all shut up, putting an end to this ridiculous pretence. Perhaps Bart has come to the same conclusion and, unlike me, has put the theory into practice.

The Volvo turns onto Church Road and begins to climb the hill. 'Do we need to stop at your house first?' he asks me.

'No,' Kamala says. 'She does not. The gardener is there and is perfectly capable of babysitting.'

'It is only his first day,' I say. 'Perhaps –'

'Ella, don't be an enabler,' she says.

'Wife, don't be a bully,' he says. 'Ella?'

With fists clenched so tightly that my closely-clipped fingernails are digging into my palms, I say, 'Thank you, but it's fine. Drop us off at the path.'

'Good girl,' she says.

I don't feel good. I'm far from a wicker basket. Guilty. Selfish. Resigned. Despite the fact that my husband has never once asked me to keep a watchful eye over him. Never once has he threatened he would end it all if I stayed out too long. Nor has he ever begged for me to remain his wife. If I left him he might bear it as he has everything else. The endless blame swirling around him like a cyclone, funnelling out any belief that he can be loved. That he deserves love.

'How can you love me?' he has asked.

'How can you ask that?' I have said. But the truth is, I'm no longer certain I do. There is love, yes, but is it actually for this man, or is it for the man he used to be?

The therapist continually reminds me – perhaps it is more a reproach – that if my husband was capable of feeling better, he would. That Bart also wishes to cast off his gloom. I've been given stacks of reading on the subject, again by the therapist, all echoing this sentiment that depression is a disease that no one seeks. That it is a completely different matter altogether from simply wallowing.

The therapist was appalled when I asked, 'If this is the case, then why doesn't Bart try to be better? There are medications he could look into. He could at least put effort into making small goals, like to shower. Or something. He has given up.'

This earned me an hour-long lecture on my ignorance and insensitivity.

Have I not also lost? I thought.

Thad pulls the car up at the corner where the golf estate flows into the protected fynbos. The muted greens and browns fold along the descending hills, where the ocean bashes the cliffs, creating a distant, rhythmic boom. Thad gets out and goes over to the passenger side to help his wife. He hands her the rucksack, holding the straps while she threads her arms through.

'I'll carry that,' I say.

'No, I'm doing this,' she says. 'Besides, shouldn't you also be carrying something?'

I'm confused. Our water and light snack are in the very rucksack she is refusing to hand over. She nods towards the car, her eyes narrowing until they resemble arrows. There, on the backseat of the Volvo, is my camera, tucked inside its small padded case. I take the camera out and slip it across my chest, the case slung over a shoulder.

'Don't you need a hiking stick or something?' I say.

'No hen-pecking, Ella,' she says.

Thad chuckles, plants a kiss on his wife's lips and drives off. A flock of francolins with hatchlings scatters in his wake, filling the air with squawks of protest. I pick up my camera as they dive behind a large aloe, the babies following the noise of the mothers. I glance through the lens, playing with the settings while considering the light.

Gently taking my hand, Kamala says, 'Let's walk a bit. Relax.'

Hand in hand we head down the path, following the palisade fence. It lines three sides of the golf estate. The fourth side is left open to the fynbos. I suppose should break-ins occur it is a matter of what the thief can confidently carry while dodging the snakes.

I lift my chin. The November sun is kind today, brushing the skin with soft heat. The breeze is light, soothing, stirring the air just enough to prevent it from going stale. A welcome break from the relentless wind that has been bellowing for the past few weeks. A sugarbird darts by, diving low into a protea. Another marble in my gut begins to dissolve as we reach the Cape St. Blaize trail. I turn towards the lighthouse, which sits about three kilometres away to our left.

'No,' she says, with a slight tug to my hand. 'I have an idea.' A dreamy smile spreads across her face

'What do you mean?'

A dash of devilish humour invades; she smirks. 'We are going to be daring today.'

Unearthing my camera felt daring. Yet all I say is: 'How so?'

'Your coriander has given me a plan.'

I dutifully follow without protest as she leads downwards, at an angle, away from the lighthouse, our supposed goal for this morning's walk. A moment of curiosity invades, 'Where are we headed?'

She stomps a hiking boot, sending up a puff of dust. I watch it rise over the laces of her boots before it gives itself up to gravity. Like Bart, trying to emerge from bed.

'We are heading,' she says, 'to my rock place. I adore it and have decided you must see it too. Then we will go to the lighthouse.'

I nod and we continue walking, as if her answer has proved to be satisfactory. In actual fact, I have no clue what the rock place is, or how far we must walk to reach it. I seldom explore these paths.

I keep my wanderings closer to the beach where the water can lick my feet. It brings me comfort, a sense of connection that I cannot obtain from the dusty cliff tops of botanical wonders, residing in constant thirst. Up here I find myself amongst this hardy vegetation wondering what it must be like to look down upon such a large body of water, perpetually out of reach. It must be maddening to be a plant, unable to seize vital resources, forced to sit and wait for life itself to come to you. Unless you are Bart, who might be rather content if he were to turn into an olive tree, whose twisted, gnarled branches tell a tale of long-lived anguish.

'You are the only person I know who has to be near the water but will not go in it,' Bart said, early in our relationship.

A lazy observance, inaccurate in its simplicity. I have always swum, while trying the patience of countless instructors for my refusal to submerge my head. I would perform any stroke required on my back or swim on my belly with my head poking out like a puppy. It is not about like or dislike or fear. It's a matter of trust.

Water is wild and untamed. Its placid nature on a calm day can lull people into forgetting about the powerful undertow lurking for prey. A delightful little stream may one day transform into a raging flood, tearing down fence posts and rocking foundations. We may gratefully gulp water into our bodies for health. But water will willingly shove itself down any open portal. Water cannot choke a toe or break through my knee, but it can pound the air from the lungs, or stuff itself through the nostrils, force its way down the oesophagus.

'Yes, but then there are people,' Luxolo once said. 'A man may kiss and stroke his lover in one moment, then bruise and choke her in another. With anything in life, there are no guarantees.'

Is it so hard to believe that the essence that composes seventy-percent of a human body would share the same complex, contrary nature? 'Even so,' I'd said, 'I still see no reason to stick my head into the jaws of my son's killer.'

'To find peace,' Luxolo had said.

I am not sure if peace is truly possible, even in death. Perhaps that is why I have not joined my husband in his slow decay. Whereas my son, in death, is now rejoining the living, teaspoon by teaspoon.

A squeeze of my hand brings my attention back to Kamala. We can no longer comfortably walk side by side. She steps forward, taking command of our route. I follow dutifully behind, noticing how the path narrows almost in accordance to the gradient. Is this the natural occurrence with trails not regularly tended?

I look up and study my friend's back. Early this morning, before making my way to the beach, I'd vowed to make an effort today. To be social. That if I expected Bart to emerge from our home and attend a meeting – to engage with the human race – then so must I. To place the burden of conversation on others is, in a way, making yourself more important than another. A method of closing myself off despite stepping outside the gate.

I clear my throat. 'Would you say that this path is following an exponential equation?'

My friend lets out a light, easy laugh, cooling my anxiety. 'Ah,' she says, 'I've heard this one. That people really don't invent anything, but simply recreate what is already there. Like the helicopter being inspired by hummingbirds.'

'Precisely.'

'Are you suggesting that nature is the first professor of maths?'

'I think people have already suggested as much, as you pointed out with the bird. But I'm asking if this path is also following mathematical rules?'

She glances down and toes the sand. 'Maybe, given gravity and all that. Why?'

I smile, refusing to admit that I began this conversation with no other purpose than to have started one. But now that I have, there is a deep yearning to say more. 'I simply find it puzzling how we humans behave erratically despite living amidst such order.'

'I am not sure I would go so far as to call nature orderly. Things do happen. Like, I may know that statistically a shark attack is near impossible, but you're still not going to catch me on a surfboard.'

'Then perhaps our erratic behaviour is only in the micro. In the macro we do behave fairly predictably: eat, sleep, defecate, and reproduce.'

Kamala stops and turns slightly towards me, taking care not to overbalance. 'War,' she says. 'That is against nature on the grandest scale.'

'But don't you think maths is how war is able to be so grand?

The technology required to make such an impact all boils down to maths.'

'Maybe.' She squints, as if she is mulling this over.

'And what about hurricanes and earthquakes? That is a bit like earth's version of war. Are earthquakes mathematical?'

Kamala gives me a slight frown. 'The next time I take you walking with me, I'm insisting you wear a hat.'

I give her a small smile, while my insides churn with mild embarrassment. I suppose I did get rather carried away.

'Then again,' she says with a grin, 'you might have a point. Right now, however, I'm just glad that today, thanks to mathematics or random luck, is gorgeous and you and I get to walk in it.' With that, she proceeds along the path. I follow, admiring how her movements radiate a deep pleasure. Nobody ever doubts that Kamala is happy to be alive.

An ignorant person would believe that Kamala can be who she is because she has never known grief. But that is not true. Ten years ago her eldest brother died. He had been training for the Cape Argus Cycle Race. Witnesses say the bakkie veered into the verge. It hit her brother, then careened on, half mounted on the pavement, for a hundred metres, before suddenly crossing back over two lanes and disappearing down a side road. They never caught the driver, in all likelihood a drunk. It was a terrible, inexplicable and pointless tragedy.

The whole family grieved: parents, grandparents, cousins, Kamala and her remaining brother and sister. Yet, despite the pain, their lives did not stop with his death. All three children went on to further education, married. The grandparents and cousins attended graduations, weddings and continued to mark birthdays with festivities. Her father, an attorney, maintained his successful practice. Her mother never allowed her home to collapse into a state of neglect. And Kamala can still find pleasure in the simple things. Coriander. Real butter.

Once, during a visit to Mossel Bay, Kamala's mother mentioned that had she not lost a son, she might have resisted the idea of her daughter marrying a Greek. 'Loss teaches you what is important,' she said.

Those words haunt me. What does this world have to offer Bart? I want to argue his choice is wrong. But here I am, trying to sell myself the notion that this – hiking in the soft November sun – is why it is worth carrying on.

*

I warily eye the waves, battling to gain entry against a series of boulders and outcrops. An army's last stand. Eerie. 'Are we below sea level?' I ask.

Kamala shrugs. 'I'm not sure. Although, if you climb up that far side and peep over, you can see that the water is already fairly deep. In fact, I've spotted whales hanging out there.'

I take a step back.

'Relax,' she laughs. 'Seriously, I've never seen a wave breach those rocks. Ever. I promise.'

The rock place is like being at the bottom of a grey bowl. I glance back at the bank we've recently descended. A trickle of fresh water slogs its way through the greedy foliage until it reaches a flat slab of rocks, spreading out as if someone spilt her drink. Drip, drip, drip, it feeds into the grey stones below. Does this water eventually reach the sea, only a hundred or so metres away, or do the stones suck the moisture out?

Kamala scrambles up a small bank, towards the mouth of a cave. Her feet are sure, her hands confident of holds, she moves without pause or slip.

Kamala turns her head slightly. 'Come on. I want to show you something.'

I stick my toe into a foothold and shove up. My knee bashes against an unyielding surface. I bite back my cry. It is too humiliating to be struggling after a pregnant woman made it to the top without mishap. She sticks out a hand. I shake my head. 'No, I'm fine.'

'Your ancestors were clearly flatlanders. But I suppose not everyone's people wandered the Himalayans.'

Standing at the top I begin to smack the dust from my jeans. 'Really? For some reason I always thought your ancestors had come from India's more southern regions.'

'Well, technically speaking that is where they boarded the boat. But it is totally possible that back in the Stone Age they lived further north. Who's to say?'

I let out a small laugh.

Kamala takes my hand, 'Come, this way.'

A huge sense of relief fills me as we pass the cave without entering. These hollows beneath the earth's crust are far more daunting than forcing my head under the water. What if the earth was to yawn, the cave to collapse?

'You are the most claustrophobic person I've ever met,' Bart once said.

'I simply like room to breathe.'

'Caves have air.'

'It is not of the right quality. Some people insist on only drinking the best vintages. I like the freest of air.'

'Free range air? Like chickens?'

'Precisely.'

'And you make fun of me for not wanting to scuba dive.' He rolled his eyes heavenward, before pulling me into his arms with a kiss.

There is a second cave ahead, but Kamala turns inward, entering an open amphitheatre full of golden northern sunlight. The stones in this cup gleam, radiating a soul-deep warmth that does not stifle. She stops and smiles. 'This is where Thaddeus and I first made love.'

I nod, having no words for this sort of conversation. Not information I ever thought I needed. Nor am I convinced I need to know this now. I suppose I should at least be curious. Although I've never felt the urge to share with anyone where Bart and I first made love. It is a wonderful memory. But I am selfish; I want it all to myself. Sadly, it may be that I got my wish, more than I ever truly desired. Is Bart able to recall such a moment of us?

'So here is my plan,' she says. 'If you can bear it, I want to have photos done in the nude. I wasn't kidding when I said I have no idea what to give Thad for Christmas.'

What's wrong with a bottle of ouzo, I think. Instead I say, 'Not showing these to your future offspring, I suppose?'

'Certainly not. But your idea has convinced me that I should start a tradition of marital porn, and there is no time like the present.'

'Erotica.'

She settles her clothed self on a rock and daintily crosses her heavily clad feet. 'Is there a difference between porn and erotica?'

'Beauty,' I say.

'Porn stars can be beautiful.' A slight pink tints her cheeks.

I confess I had never considered her to be the type of woman to watch porn. Then again, what sort of person do I imagine watches porn? Bart and I had watched it, on occasion. He had a knack of finding videos that did not feel threatening or aggressive or misogynistic.

'Is this the sort of stuff you watched while at varsity?' I once asked him.

'No.'

'Then what kind was it?'

'Ella,' he'd said with a pained look, 'I was young and immature. I've grown. Let's leave it at that.'

Kamala is still waiting for an answer. She has this look she does with her eyes. They widen, but without bewilderment or innocence. Keep talking, those wide eyes demand.

I exhale slowly. 'Porn only has one aim, arousal—or release, if you will.'

She nods, as if I were explaining the latest tax reforms.

'So because of this, the poses in porn – or even the story line, should there be one – are strictly related to this one goal of culminating physical pleasure.'

She nods again. Not a hint of embarrassment. My cheeks,

however, are heating up at a dramatic rate, and unlike Kamala's flattering tinted blushes, I'll be bright red.

'Right, so then with erotica the idea is to be sensual, sexual, but with its main aim beauty or perhaps art. For example, a nude woman turned away from the camera, in a slightly modest pose, can be beautiful yet invoke a sexual response for precisely what she is not displaying. When trying to take erotic photographs, the key is nuance. When done well, even a single picture will create a complex reaction.'

'Yes,' she says, shaking her finger at me. 'That's what I want. Arty pictures.'

I clear my throat, waiting to see what she means.

She takes off her jacket, placing it neatly on a rock, then draws out her scarf, coiling it carefully on top of the jacket. She grabs the hem of her top and pauses. 'So you are okay with this, yes?'

I blink a few times, brain unwilling to articulate an answer, but somehow my head bobs up and down.

She beams, raising the hem, revealing an expanse of taut, smooth flesh.

I start to look away, but then stop, reminding myself that I have photographed subjects in the nude before. Never a person I knew so well, however. This is the first time I have seen my friend topless. A part of me is fascinated. It's her skin. It possesses a sheen, a youthful glow, that defies her age and is testimony to her vigour. One would never guess that she is actually six months my senior.

'Remember, you cannot comment about my weight,' she says. 'It would be rude.'

'You are beautiful,' I say.

'It's the pregnancy glow,' she says, lowering herself down. 'You had it too.'

I fiddle with the lenses, trying to think of a reply. I do adore her for this. She never pretends Kai didn't happen. That I never experienced what she is now experiencing. Most people seem to believe that I should agree simply to act as though Kai never occurred, for their comfort. The polite, well-mannered, thing to do.

'I think you are confused,' I say, lowering the camera. 'I was a sweaty pile, not a glowing beauty. But who's to say, there are no photographs.'

She gasps, awkwardly frozen over shoelaces. 'Why not?'

I shrug.

'So you avoided those "this is my belly at five months" and all that?'

I nod.

'But you were happy, right?' A boot is set beside her jacket.

'Yes, of course. We had wanted a baby. Heavens, Bart was the proudest father-to-be you've ever seen aside from Thad. I was thrilled to finally be pregnant.'

'Being happy about having a baby and enjoying pregnancy are not the same.'

'Very true.'

She points a sock at me. 'So was your pregnancy so miserable you couldn't take a single self-portrait?'

I give her a soft smile. 'It wasn't that.'

'But not one photo?'

'Not one.'

'Damn. If I had known that I'd have gotten out my point-and-shoot and snapped a few. Don't you regret it?' She flings off her last boot and wiggles her toes, painted in a charming lilac.

I'm about to ask if she managed to paint her toes herself, when she abruptly stands, shoving down her trousers and tosses them on the pile. She is now unapologetically naked. For a moment all I do is stare, admiring her body, the way her long dark hair spills around her heavy breasts. She does not flinch. It is apparent that if some random man stumbled onto this scene, this woman before me wouldn't cover herself up. She'd look the intruder right in the eye and he would find himself apologising for being so thoughtless as to have wandered down a public path.

'Perfect,' I say. With a tilt of my hips the frame moves into position, the lens adjusts and the shutter button is clicked. I will take many photographs, but this is the one Thad will love. He will know this woman.

'You didn't answer my question,' she says.

'About what?' I tilt my head. Click.

'Do you regret not taking any pregnancy pics?'

I shift my weight to the left. A bird cries overhead. Click. 'No,' I say.

'Hmm.' She glances up, sending hair cascading down her back. The curve is perfect.

Click.

This will be Thad's second favourite. I could stop now, but Kamala would be insulted. There is a fine line between getting a subject relaxed in front of the camera, and a person becoming too familiar with the lens. It is that brief period in between that a person's mettle may shine through the lie of memory.

Memories do not photograph easily; photographs merely project what we wish our memories to be. Even in my most camera-dependent days I knew this. A photograph imprisons a piece of time, the length of a shutter click. These still images warp time to fit into that one photograph; a two-hour party becomes reduced to a split second. 'What a good time,' people say, despite harsh words, a late guest and the poor crème brûlée. An entire life encapsulated in one portrait. 'Such a wonderful man,' people say, despite his penny-pinching, excessive drinking and off-colour jokes.

We all carry moments of triumph and utter foolishness. Does anyone defecate with dignity?

What memories does a picture of a pregnant woman provide? The fact that she gained weight? They rarely have anything original to add, only slotted into a frame etched with saccharine clichés. These photographs of Kamala only work because Kamala allows so much of who she is to be on display. The belly is the least of it.

Which was precisely my problem with photographing my own pregnancy. An identity crisis of a sort, but far less dramatic. Perhaps others have experienced it too: this bizarre feeling of trying to *be yourself* while being occupied by something else that didn't always feel like *somebody else*. At times I felt so lonely, even while the pregnancy meant I was never truly alone. That through the elation and seemingly endless drudgery, there was this companionship – everything done together – with an individual-to-be that seemed bonded to me, intimately known to me, while at the same time a complete stranger. How does one photograph that?

Yet I was never him; and Kai, even after he was born, wasn't fully Kai. Birth was another step towards *becoming* Kai. The first thing that made him laugh, the first words, the first time he disliked one food but adored another. He was emerging. Solidifying. And from the moment he first took a breath, the camera could begin to make sense of it. Still, I could not record the first time he had a complete thought. Was that when he first came to *be*? Because it seemed that even on the day he died, there remained so much more to him to *be* that never happened. Yet he was who he was. Can we lose what we do not have?

A photograph can convey emptiness, but it is never empty. It holds something. But not necessarily what matters. Precisely why it was so frustrating to be unable to photograph Bart's awareness of Friday. What is a day of the week? Even placing a calendar on a desk circling 'Monday' is not actually photographing Monday. Besides, it could be a lie. Yes, it says Monday; but perhaps the owner of the desk has been absent, or too lazy to keep track of the week.

Captions. They are supposed to take over where the photograph leaves off. But the truth is, those are usually fiction. A story, with illustrations, much like the calendar on the desk. With so much potential for untruths, one may as well trust faulty memories. At least those memories are mine, and mine alone.

*

'Didn't realise you could get reception here,' Kamala says, as my cell phone rings.

'Progress, apparently,' I say, fishing the phone from my pocket.

We've only just hiked out of the rock place and hit the actual St. Blaize trail. How long has somebody been trying to reach us? Worst-case scenarios swirl until I see the caller's ID. It is the therapist. The panic thickens into a marble and drops solidly into place with its mates.

'Good morning,' he says.

'Is it?' I say.

'Ella,' he says. 'I am here with Bart and we both feel it would best if he goes to the meeting himself.'

A fly lands on my thigh. I swipe at it and miss. 'He is going to drive?' The fly buzzes furiously in my face.

'Oh no, I will drive. But this is something he needs to do on his own.'

I take another swipe. Missed. 'You mean without me.'

'I beg your pardon.'

'Well,' I say, turning away from the fly, 'he obviously isn't doing this alone if you are there. It is only my presence you are objecting to.' I don't know what has possessed me to say this. They are useless, argumentative words. I have heard this all before. The therapist intervenes on something planned. He informs me how it will now be carried out. At the last moment Bart claims he needs more time. The therapist reiterates that we must respect Bart's needs. My husband returns to bed.

'Ella,' he says.

I wait.

The man inhales loudly. I imagine a hot air balloon filling up, readying for take-off. He says, 'Once again, you are failing to appreciate that…'

I can give the speech myself. That I must understand that there is a difference between the relationship between a patient and the therapist, and between the patient and his spouse. It is imperative that these lines are not blurred, crossed or mistaken for the same sort of relationship.

It has been made clear that my opinion, as Bart's spouse – the person that actually has to handle his dreadfully vile boxer shorts and coax him to wash his own body – does not carry any meaningful weight or insight because I am *too close to the situation*. Once, when I was feeling particularly irate, I replied to such a statement with, 'Yes, I am so very close to the situation that I can assure you it really does stink, in the most literal sense.'

Today, however, I only listen.

Kamala tries to snatch the phone away, but I wave her off. 'Hang up,' she says. The words come out in a hiss. I think of the snakes lurking in the fynbos.

'Hang! Up!' Kamala's face is bloating with anger.

'Is someone there?' He sounds mildly bemused. I have often suspected that despite his dire warnings of negative co-dependent relationships, in his mind I have no other worth than acting as Bart's captive crutch.

'Yes, actually there is,' I say.

'Oh, well I do apologise *if* I have interrupted something important.'

It is his emphasis on the 'if' that causes Old Ella to take control of the phone. 'Thank you, because *you* have.'

Ella, there is no need for such a tone. I know Bart's recovery is of the utmost importance to you and thought you would appreciate being kept up to date on his progress. But perhaps we can discuss this at a time when you are less distracted.'

Old Ella is furious. She vows that as soon as she is home she will change the pass code to the gate. She will tell the man he is no longer welcome in her home. She will research new doctors and make Bart understand that this is for the best. In fact, it is time. 'Dr Evans, you have dropped by my home unannounced and uninvited and taken it upon yourself to change our day's plans without consulting me. Yes, *our* plans.'

'Now Ella, this is what Bart wants and needs. I can tell you require some time to digest the fact that this is not about you. We will speak again later. Good day.'

He hangs up. Old Ella wants to phone him right back and set him straight. But the Ella-of-today is too exhausted, too bereft, too beaten. This is only the beginning. We have been here before. By noon it will be over: Bart will not go to the meeting today.

Kamala lays a gentle hand on my arm. 'I'm proud of you.'

I can barely nod.

She gives my arm a squeeze. 'Is he really a doctor?'

'I have no idea. He can't prescribe meds, but it could be possible that he holds a doctorate in something.'

'A PhD in bullshit?'

I give a weak smile as my legs slowly give out. My body sinks until it is sitting on the dark sandy soil. I take a deep breath and release it slowly while my watering eyes scan the view laid out before me. The ocean is sparkling under the sunlight, as if a child ran across it with glitter. The smell of the spring fynbos is fresh and clean. The day has presented such magnificence, yet it is already spoilt.

The rot creeps up, through the earth and presses against my jeans, slowly working its way through the threads until it reaches my skin. My epidermis has no defence against this disease. My immune system is helpless as the rot breaches the soft tissue and spreads, seeking out the circulatory system, the marrow of my bones.

This is how Bart feels, I think.

'Ella?'

Kamala's voice is fading. I hear a curse. It seems further away, as if I am falling into myself. My eyes remain locked on the glittering sea. From up here the individual waves are undetectable; the water appears as smooth as an ironed bed sheet. A part of me begins to believe I could stride out onto the blue surface and walk across the bay. That is exactly how Bart surfed. He never doubted the water under his board, just as I never question the earth supporting my feet as I take my next step. Bart used to glide across that water with as much confidence and grace as any dancer on stage. There was this certainty, fluidity, to his movements that made it look as if he knew exactly where he was going. I had always assumed that he was the strong one.

I feel Kamala sink next to me. 'Ella?'

'Need a moment.' My words come out in a whisper.

Her body hovers briefly before rising. My eyes have not strayed. The glitter burns through the pupil, attacking the retina. It is a hot light. It was the same when I was watching Bart work. The fire in the furnace, the blowtorch, light radiating from the molten glass. It is both magnificent and frightening. Yet Bart never appeared intimidated. He created in the same manner as he surfed: moving alongside the fire, the glass, the instruments with poise, willing everything to behave. As if it had no other choice but to glide along with his vision. He had a way of focusing, shutting out everything else so that, at times, I felt like an invader witnessing a private act.

He was never a man who could multi-task. Each self-assured movement was executed completely. When I lay beneath him, feeling his touch, I truly believed that I was the most important person in his world. Making love with Bart was an intense experience that left me feeling thoroughly adored. But I should have known, or understood better, that I was not his everything. It was clear from how he surfed that I was not with him, not present in any semblance. Out there on the water there was only him, the board and the sea. It was the same with his work. I suspect even his partners lose their humanity in Bart's eyes as he creates. These men he loves melt into another tool along with the blowtorch, the newspapers, the vice.

I wonder in Bart's grief if he actually sees Kai. Does he grieve for the smell of Kai's head, after he tumbled in the grass, after he rolled in the sand? Does Bart remember how smooth Kai's skin felt, plump with newness no cream can create? Does he remember our son's laugh? It was a sound unlike any other; it shimmered with lightness and pure joy. Or does Bart only see his old cell phone?

The cell phone had sat in the palm of his hand. It had looked harmless enough. Just a typical phone, black, nothing special about it. Everyone has one, even the poor in this country. Nor are they objects of fear, like a knife or a gun. Even so, I was adamant that he shouldn't use it.

'They're fine,' I had said, revelling in the moment. 'Leave them.' I was a woman out with her lover, not a mother pawed by small hands of ceaseless need.

'I won't be long,' he had said.

The waiter came by the table. 'May I take the plate?'

I'd smiled, the taste of the ostrich pâté still lingering on my palate. What luxury to have time to savour an appetiser. 'Yes, thank you.'

'Just a quick call,' Bart had said, springing up from his seat, fingers gripping around the phone. A brief kiss on my lips. 'You know she hasn't really ever looked after a child on her own. Even me.'

'She'd have called if there was a problem,' I'd said, laughing. He always said I fussed too much. But there he was, already wanting to check-in, well before dessert.

He popped outside. I twirled my wine glass between my fingertips. I took a sip. How long was he actually out there? At the time it felt like only a minute or two, although in reality it was more like five or six. Time had flittered away, as if there would always be more, while I sipped that wine oblivious to what my future held. I still remember how free I felt, gloriously liberated from the handcuffs of overprotective parenting for the first time in almost two years.

Bart returned. He placed the phone on the table and gave me a sheepish smile. 'They're fine,' he'd said.

'Of course, they are' I had said.

'But in my defence, she was anxious. Wanted me to go over the whole bedtime routine again.'

We'd laughed at his mother's ridiculousness. Eyes sparkling, we'd raised our glasses, toasting one another over the soft candlelight. Such upmarket atmosphere; the Milkwood Cottage Cuisine was fine dining at its best.

The cell began to vibrate as the waiter set down Bart's dinner of roast lamb. He picked it up on the second buzz. Phone pressed to his ear, I watched in confusion as colour peeled from his face. Then without a word, the cell phone crashed onto the table. Again. And again. I was aware of the waiter, stunned, by my side. My plate hovering in his outstretched hand, bearing the catch-of-the-day, as pieces of screen were imbedded into new potatoes, spiked into upturned glasses of wine.

'I'd only left him in the bath for a few minutes,' she had said. 'Just a few minutes, to answer the phone.'

*

Kamala grasps my hand. 'Come,' she says. 'Thad is going to meet us at the top.'

Startled, I look up. My vision blurs, fades, having stared into the bright light far too long. A steady thrum presses against my temples. 'We need to reach the lighthouse.'

'No, we don't need to. It was only an idea. Forget it.'

I shake my head. The pressure on my temples flares until it stabs the base of my skull creating a firework of pain. 'Please, I'm fine.'

She kneels down in front of me. 'No, you're not. But that's okay. At least you try. Now, let's go.'

I blindly tug her down next to me, for once not taking care of her extra burden. There are no words of protest. Her hand settles on my back. The strokes are smooth, firm, without urgency.

'You don't need to do that,' I say.

'I know,' she says, and her hand continues to move. Hair is brushed from my face, locks tucked behind my ear.

'You're fussing,' I say.

'Yes,' she says. 'I am.'

Her fingers creep up my neck, the thumb pressing into the base of the skull. The pain hovers for a beat then begins to recede like the tide. 'Ella,' she says. 'Tell me something.'

'What.' It comes out harshly, snappishly. I didn't mean it like that. I attempt to look her in the eye despite the fuzzy vision. But her gentle touch does not project annoyance.

'When are you going to start taking care of you? Honestly, I know I keep saying it. But it's time. It's his choice, now. You can't help him until he wants to be helped.'

'I hired a gardener.'

'Yes, you did.'

The fingers begin to tug on my hair. The sensation reminds me of a weaverbird arranging its nest. The males are always slightly frantic, in competition with one another, trying to woo a mate. When they fail, the despondent male knocks the nest down to try, try again until he reaches his goal, or no females remain.

My eyes begin to focus; my shoelaces gain distinct edges. Steadier, I say, 'I took photos today, and you know, I actually enjoyed it. For a moment I was focused, in a rhythm. It was as if…'

'You knew of nothing else.'

'Yes.'

Her fingers press on my skull, running downwards, pulling the blood through. New blood rushes to replace the old, as if she has willed my circulatory system to continue onwards. She heaves herself to her feet. It is an awkward, jerking movement, clumsy, so unlike her normal grace.

I peer up at her. 'I so badly wanted him to make that meeting at noon.'

'I know,' she says, reaching down and grasping my wrist. 'I know.' She yanks me to my feet. 'I know.'

Perhaps she does. Perhaps she wanted the same.

My feet drag themselves up the incline. But now my eyes hone in on the cigarette butts ground into the sandy soil; the plastic packets lurking in the undergrowth caught up in dry scraggly branches; the broken bottles, with their sharp ragged ends poking up near flat rocks, stained with traces of human excrement. The boom of the ocean is ominous.

Thad is there, at the top, as promised. His face has lost its customary easy smile. Leaning against the car, arms folded over his chest, is a man purposefully neutral. Wordlessly he opens the rear door.

'I'll walk,' I say.

Ignoring me, he reaches out and takes his wife's hand, and helps her into the car. He lets me go a few paces before calling over his shoulder: 'Your car is still parked at the café.'

I stop. Emotional pleas are tedious and wearing, but I can still cope with logic. There is nothing more to say. Thad holds the door open, waiting patiently as I slide into the back. The door shuts. Silence. The driver side door opens. Thad enters. He shuts the door. Nothing but the click of seatbelts. My fingers clench, waiting for the first comment, the first murmur of assurance. Instead, with the twist of the key, the CD player comes on, filling the car with sound mid-song. Such tact. As if it *just so happened* to already be playing. Most people would have flipped it on as we pulled away, punctuating the awkwardness.

Or brought up the weather.

But my friends have far too much finesse.

Gratitude swallows me as the Volvo descends. A parade of homes whisks past. I wait for the anger, but it does not arrive. Perhaps I said what needed to be said to the therapist. Now I am only left with what it is. This place, an emotional bowl, that Bart and I seem incapable of scaling. The sadness sits upon my lap and becomes.

I could leave. Choices. He made his. I have yet to make mine. Or perhaps staying is a choice. I keep waiting, as if something might happen. But all that happens is what is happening. If that isn't something, then I need to do something. But what? What I wanted is here. Or was.

Amazing how doing so little can use up so much energy.

Perhaps, to Bart, I have become one of the numerous security fences that line these streets. I keep his life at bay: taking the calls, the emails, the bill paying. It is such a façade. As if we all agreed the worst danger lives elsewhere. Security is making Barts of many of us.

There is such a variety of ways to do it: bars and spikes, bamboo topped with razor wire and solid walls with slick coats of paint adorned with viciously sharp metal ivy. The trend for coloured palisade is most bemusing. Many seem to believe that by making the bars green the fence will blend in with the lawn. It doesn't. One person has gone for copper. It is the better of the two looks. Ours was installed years ago due to my mother-in-law's fear of a pony snatch. The bare metal is set between concrete pillars whose white paint is peeling. It adds to the Miss Havisham air.

A few properties have framed their entrance gates with towering pedestals boasting enormous African Eagles, cast in concrete. They glare down their beaks, as if they can radiate lasers from their beady eyes. One property has a large stone lion lurking to the side, as if in the shadows it might be mistaken for the real thing.

Many years ago I made Bart sit astride the stone lions on Rhodes Memorial, which looms above Cape Town from the mountain's base. 'Now I feel like true colonialist spawn,' he'd said.

'You are.'

He gave me a wry smile.

Click.

I still have the photograph. We'd laughed so much that day, at ourselves, at the world's history and continued idiocy.

I can't hear the memory of Bart's laughter, anymore. The real kind, not a scornful mock or grim guffaw. Yet, I still hear Kai's. A bit.

Thad pulls into the private driveway of Plato's Bru. I step out into Kamala's arms. Her hard stomach pushes into mine. I suck my belly in.

'Speak soon,' she says.

Wordlessly I give her a kiss on the cheek. A backwards wave to Thad. They let me go.

The air of the Prius is stuffy, aged. It strikes my nostrils, prickles my skin. Hastily, I lower the window as my stomach rolls.

A dark head with tight curls sleeked with grease pops into the frame. A grin, teeth stained and broken, 'Môre, mevrou.'

He holds out cupped hands, knuckles so raw they are blistering pink. He smells exactly like Bart when he has not showered for a week: a putrid sweetness mixed with undertones of sour sweat. The filth is piteously contrasted with the straight-out-of-the-pack yellow car guard bib strapped across the chest.

I nod, fumbling with the glove box. My fingers skate through the debris until they come in contact with a silver coin. I place it in his hand. The polite thing to do would be to say something – a hello, thank you – or, at the very least, give him a small smile. I can't.

He accepts the coin with a deferring bow, his smile now absent.

Understand, I want to say.

But why should he? How about I understand him, having to cup his hands for a coin or two and act grateful for a pittance while he stood in the November sun hour after hour with no relief. He who has to spend his day in his filthy skin, last soaked in a steaming hot bubble bath when…Well, has he ever? There are plenty of people still, to this day, who have never indulged in such a simple pleasure. A pail, a rag, scrubbing themselves standing up, piece by piece, shivering in the open air.

Yet, I want to ask him. *Understand me.*

He is still there. Framed by my window, coin vanished. What is he waiting for? I blink and then watch as his face falls into that unmistakable look of pity.

Emotion threatens to erupt. Quickly I pull the car away, gripping the steering wheel so tightly that my fingers ache. I got exactly what I silently desired, and yet I would have coped better with anger, spit in the face. Pity, it is awful, piercing my intestines, rattling the marbles.

A car door swings open. I swerve.

A cyclist speeds by. My teeth sink into my lip.

A bakkie follows. So close.

A woman with her baby tied to her back steps out into the middle of the street. I hit the brakes.

Breath whooshes from burning lungs.

How long had I forgotten to breathe?

*

The therapist is gone by the time I reach the house. I find Bart in the hammock. I stand there, discombobulated, drained, yet assuredly relieved. There is the tell-tale rhythmic rise and fall of his chest indicating he is merely asleep. A deep sleep. The kind that says, I'm not going out today.

I want to smack him. Instead, I run a finger along the frayed edges of the quilt that covers him. The blanket's scene of cheerful ponies marching along the English countryside is an eerie contrast to my husband's ghoulish pallor.

'Such a gay scene,' my mother-in-law would say about the kitsch piece.

She used the word gay at every opportunity. 'We must reclaim it,' she would say.

'Why?' I once asked.

'Because it is wrong to have a word that means happy sullied in this manner.'

'In what manner? How is it being sullied?'

'I am not having this discussion with you,' she said. 'You insist on being difficult. You should try being more gay.'

'If I were more gay, I wouldn't be married to your son.'

She had stomped out of the room with the dreadful quilt in tow. It was one of the first things I set to toss out after she died. But some soul – Bart? Happiness? – must have rescued it from the give-away pile.

I glare at the ponies. They prance in defiant delight. We're alive, they seem to whinny. Look at us! We frolic in our everlasting scene.

Dylan must have played a role in the ponies' resurrection. The quilt is laid on with too much care, the folds too precise. I cannot imagine the therapist taking upon himself to act with such tenderness. And it is most un-Bart like. The man rolls himself up into a tight chrysalis, routinely emerging with devastating results. Or he crumples upon the blankets in a manner that screams, Bring me my smelling salts.

I've long suspected that Dr. Evans revels in Bart's inability to move forward. His advice is routinely dubious. Such as his encouragement for my husband to take his rest in bed, drapes tightly drawn, as if the gloom can be contained to a single room. Surely that is not right. Is it ever advisable to encourage wallowing? And Dr Evans seems to maintain that because depression is a disease, the sufferer cannot be held accountable for anything. Yet I cannot bring myself to agree. Even if depression is a disease, that doesn't make the sufferer a saint, unable to be manipulative, morose, spiteful. How can Bart be totally without blame? Alcoholism is a disease, and those that recover are the ones forced to face the problem, not excuse it.

Bart always has an excuse.

A shot of fury bolts through my fingers. I release the quilt, and move away. The last thing either of us needs is for me to start shouting, foaming at the mouth. I tried that tactic once; it accomplished nothing. A momentary release. That had felt wonderful. But the fallout was nothing of the sort.

Must calm down. Find balance. Roaming the property, I tell myself that I was being dramatic earlier. 'You're fine,' I say, then wince. Only the deranged talk to themselves, don't they? I can cope. My life is here. We just need time.

The baby chards wave their tiny leaves. They ask, how much time?

I squish the thought. An image of green ooze spreads, as if I flattened a plump grub weaselling a hole through the soft tissues of my brain. It is finally happening. I'm going mad. Comfortably so.

I lengthen my stride, moving past the old coach shed, back towards the house. At the front I spy Dylan considering the hydrangea, pruning shears primed. Kill it, I think.

The madness lurking inside me cheers. Yes, kill it, the madness shrieks.

He glances over at me, shears dropping to his side. For a moment I fear I've spoken the words out loud.

He says, 'I thought this needed a bit taken off.'

'I believe you are correct,' I say, relieved the words sound sane.

The madness becomes practical, hatching a plan. When this man is established enough in our lives I will pay him a handsome bonus to murder this bush and take the blame for its demise. Soon, soon.

All in good time, as they say.

Oblivious to my devious thoughts, Dylan raises his shears and begins to prune. I watch, captivated by such precision. He doesn't jab or slash. It's as if he holds a picture in his head of how the hydrangea should look. Stonemasons must behave in a similar manner. Dylan steps back, as if considering his work. My gaze wanders to the lawn. The grass has lost the air of a wild savannah brimming with rats and ticks. So civilised, I suppose, as if begging to be used for gentrified picnics. The neglected flowerbeds have been weeded. The fresh soil gleaming in sifted heaps, so light and fluffy it could be folded into cake batter. I make a note to purchase mulch.

Dylan sets the shears down. Scooping up an armful of debris, he tosses it into the wheelbarrow. He gardens like I cook, cleaning as he goes.

'Have you had a cup of tea or coffee this morning?'

'No, ma'am,' he says, attention back on the bush.

Since when does a hydrangea require perfect proportion? Just obliterate the blasted thing, I think.

Snip. Snip.

'Would you like a cup? I am putting the kettle on.'

'Yes, ma'am.'

Snip. Snip.

He still doesn't look at me. I try to find patience for this man, who was bold enough to ring my gate for a job, but is currently incapable of expressing his needs. But it is a bit too much like dealing with Bart. No, Dylan. Please, no. I lean forward, trying to catch his eye. 'It's Ella. And please, do you want tea or coffee?'

'Coffee would be nice, ma'am.'

Snip. Snip.

I press my lips together and inhale through my nose, feeling nostrils flair. 'It's Ella. Please. And do you take sugar? Milk? Rusks? Toast?'

He lowers the shears and turns, back straight, head confidently at ease. Is that amusement on his face? Perhaps my words were a bit sharp. But honestly, is a straight answer too much to ask?

'I take one sugar, ma'am, and some milk,' he says. 'A rusk sounds nice. Thank you. And if I may, a glass of water.' His face now wears an unmistakably   cheeky grin.

My annoyance dissolves into relief. 'Of course. Be just a moment.'

I walk away, trying to ease the knots that have developed in my shoulders and neck. Such a ridiculous thing to get worked up over. It is, after all, his first day. We are – this house, Bart, me – a bit much to deal with. Nobody in his right mind would feel comfortable demanding anything, especially after inquiring for a job. A position that did not in fact exist until he spoke it into life. Perhaps he now regrets ringing at our gate.

As the kettle boils I lay out a tray: a glass of water, rusks, a banana and a paw-paw picked yesterday. A small paring knife is placed on top of a worn, but ironed, serviette. A tea bag is dropped into the first mug, the sugar spooned in and instant coffee granules scattered to the bottom of the second. The kettle goes off. Steaming water decanted, then the milk. The coffee is stirred first, the tea allowed to steep. The white milk swirls with the brown liquid, creating a miniature whirlpool. I spin it clockwise, then counter clockwise, before giving my own cup the same treatment.

It is hypnotic.

It is a habit.

Shortly after I began boarding school, somebody told me that water drains in a different direction in the Northern Hemisphere (counter clockwise) than it does in the Southern Hemisphere (clockwise). As a young girl spread between two halves of the globe, I was determined to see this phenomenon for myself. Every flushed toilet was examined, no plughole was allowed to drain unobserved. But the toilets didn't spin. The old cisterns at our school whooshed with great force, shoving the water through. Our toilets at home were shallow, the water swallowed with a gulp.

Nor was there any consistency in the manner water drained from plugholes. Two sinks draining side by side could easily result in one emptying in one direction while the other whirled away in the opposite. It was maddening. Gripped with obsession, I couldn't understand how so many people knew this to be true, yet I was incapable of verifying it for myself.

It was all a myth.

I have always felt a bit cheated by this revelation. It irritates, even more than when scientists snatched away Pluto's planetary status.

The liquid in the mugs gradually stills. Picking up the tray, I return outdoors. At the sound of my footsteps, Dylan looks up and sets the shears against the wall of the house, precisely. I look around; there is no obvious place to place my burden. The easiest solution is to go out to the rear stoep, but then Bart will be in our midst. I shift my weight, mulling over my options.

Dylan removes his gloves and stuffs them in a back pocket, before grabbing the wheelbarrow full of dismembered hydrangea, shoving it forward. 'Here,' he says. 'Allow me.'

Gently, he removes the burden from my arms. He places it on the wheelbarrow, balancing it on top of the tangled branches, taking care not to disturb a praying mantis clinging to the edge of the debris. This deliberate sparing of life sends pleasure licking at the tension in my shoulders. The insect does not budge, as if it assumed its life would continue. Dylan waits, despite it being obvious which mug contains coffee. I suppose a good hostess does serve the drinks, not that I ever aspired to be either a host or a well-mannered lady. Nor does Dylan qualify as a guest, per se. An employee, bequeathed. Happiness certainly doesn't wait for me to make her tea. Still, since it is his first day and since it is my house, I am sure Ms Manners would have something to say about it all. Besides, his company intrigues.

I pick up his mug. As he receives it from my proffered hands, he says, 'Thank you, ma'am.'

'Ella,' I reply, bringing my own steaming mug to my lips. Leaning against the house, I stare at the street beyond the fence. It is empty. It typically is. Given that the double plot is islanded by streets on all four sides, the lack of traffic is essential for peace. A rather odd arrangement, but commonly accepted in Mossel Bay, for reasons I've never bothered to investigate.

Most of the perimeter is obscured from watchful eyes by fruit trees and various bushes. But the wicked Southeaster has thwarted all previous efforts with this one spot near the front of the house, making the hideous hydrangea visible from the street. The easiest and quickest solution is to plant more strelitzia. But the tall faux-banana leaf is overdone in this area, and produces nothing of use. Perhaps I should breed my own strain of the perennial and name it Strelitzia Bartholomew.

'Good coffee,' Dylan says.

I glance over to see him looking perfectly content. He catches my eye.

'It's only instant,' I say.

He blows into his mug, but it can't disguise the smile lurking at the edges of his mouth. 'Still good coffee. Nice and hot.'

'Well, as long as you're enjoying it.'

'I am.' He takes a healthy mouthful and smiles broadly.

His genuine pleasure makes me wish I owned larger mugs. That I had responded to his words with better grace. 'Just say, "Thank you,"' Kamala always says. 'Why do you always apologise when there is nothing to be sorry for?'

I once read similar advice in an interview with a burlesque dancer. When asked, 'What is your least favourite part of your body?' she said, 'I refuse to bring attention to my faults. I play up my strengths and say, "Thank you," to any compliments I receive.'

Reading that article was a revelation. Here was this beautiful, alluring woman brimming with sex appeal, participating in the interview with the confidence and fortitude of a man.

In fact, I don't see Dylan apologising for himself. When he rang the gate this morning he didn't say, 'Sorry for troubling you,' as I would have. No. He simply introduced himself and stated why he was there.

I should be more like that. Swallowing my last mouthful of tea, I gesture to the tray and say, 'I'll just leave this here for when it suits.'

'That sounds fine, ma'am.'

'Ella. And I'll bring lunch out in about an hour. I'm afraid I was only planning scrambled eggs on toast.'

'Thank you.'

My foot stops on the first step. 'If there is anything you don't eat, please say.'

He eyes me over his mug. 'I eat food, ma'am.'

I start to protest then realise I am doing it again. Apologising. For fresh organic eggs from my very own chickens, which will be served on yesterday's homemade bread.

But then again, most people dislike something. Kamala has ouzo. Thad, tea. Happiness cannot bite into a raw tomato. Says they squish in her mouth and do strange things to her tongue. Bart has the same opinion of grapes, though he drinks wine with no complaint. Since Kai died, my stomach cannot bear leftover fish or meat. It makes me think of decay and worms and raw odours. Since there is no reliable way to predict if Bart will eat a meal, our diets have drifted toward the vegetarian. I cannot stand food waste. Yet it happens.

I rinse my mug at the kitchen sink. Setting it on the draining board, I peer out the window at the slumbering heap. The blanket still lies across his body exactly as before. The only change is his mouth, now gaping open like an ominous hole. His breath must be stale. My nose wrinkles. Did I remind him to brush his teeth this morning? There was the shower, the soap and the cloth, but no memory of handing over a toothbrush topped with toothpaste.

It's like my last days of Kai, chasing after him with the brush, telling him to open his mouth, then demanding he open wider: *just a bit more, come on now, we're almost done.*

I shake my head. None of this matters, anymore. Bart has made his point. It jabs into parts of my heart that remain tender. With all the scars it should be a rough calloused mess, the arteries calcifying. Perhaps I should take up smoking. Then late at night the ashes could fall onto the hardwood floors and put us out of our misery.

'A tragic accident,' people will say. 'Such a shame.'

That is, after all, what they said after Kai died. Things rarely change.

I pull out my cell and ring Luxolo.

At his answer I say, 'I'm afraid Bart isn't coming.'

'I know. Kamala phoned.' He sounds resigned. Guilt engulfs me, urging me to apologise, but the energy to do so is not there.

Silence fills the space between us, running down the streets of Mossel Bay. The source of our woe continues to sleep, oblivious. Perhaps there is no need for smoking. A pillow over the face would do, and less mess. A good chance he wouldn't struggle. Might even thank me with his last pocket of air. I could bury him in the hammock, like the sailors once did. Add a weight or two near the feet, wrap it all tight, before stitching the cloth together and tossing the whole lot overboard. It would be liberating. Of course, I would first have to acquire a boat.

'Listen Ella,' Luxolo says, 'We'll work it out. Don't worry. '

I suppress a sigh. To worry, to not worry, these are not things one can or cannot do in the same way one can choose to walk or not walk, to eat or not eat. Don't worry? It is like asking somebody not to think. Perhaps that is Bart's problem. I am asking him to stop grieving, to stop obsessing about the cell phone. Maybe he simply can't, as sure as he cannot stop his heart from remembering to beat.

'Ella? Can you hear me?'

'I met Dylan.' The words pop out, rushing forwards to quell the worry in his voice.

'Ah, I wondered if he would catch up with you.'

'So it was you.'

'Hey, the man needed a job, and if you were honest with yourself, you could use a bit of help maintaining that property. The guy can fix anything.'

I think of the lawnmower, the offer to build a new compost bin, the work that has already been accomplished while I was out for a mere handful of hours. Skilled hands, creative, full of initiative. Anger contracts my blood vessels. The solution to a major problem is busy pruning a hydrangea. 'You imbecile. Why didn't you give him a job? Even if we can get Bart to work, it will only be for a few hours.'

Luxolo chuckles, but I detect a note of sadness lurking behind the mirth. 'Hey now Ella, take a breath. I did offer to hire him.'

'And?'

'He told me, and I quote, "I'm not working in an inferno. I've already been to Hell and I'm not going back."'

Fury deflates as guilt storms in. My brain begins recalling the horrific news stories and testimonials of those fleeing the interior. Those gut-wrenching tales of unfathomable woe. 'His name isn't really Dylan, is it?'

'Not exactly. But if he wanted you to know who he was or where he came from he would tell you.' He sighs. 'Ella, just let it go. He won't hurt you, he just likes his privacy and working outdoors.'

I don't reply.

'Listen, I've got to go,' he says. 'See you at three, right?'

For a moment all I see is water crashing over my head, pushing me lower and lower into the dark depths where sunlight cannot penetrate. I shudder. Swallow. Deep breath. 'Yes. See you then. Keep well.'

'You too, Ella. You too.'

Silence.

I gaze out the window at my slumbering husband. Not a flicker of movement. Perhaps Bart has a valid point. His actions articulating what his words could not. What can this man offer today that would be of any use to his partners? He is too weak. Even if he rose out of that hammock at this precise moment, casting off the dark beast that imprisons him, the physical body would still require time to heal. His thin arms are not able to bear the weight of the thick stack of newspapers. His partners should have accepted that well before today. They should have started training another pair of hands months ago. Where was our foresight?

Did the therapist anticipate any of this? If so, why didn't he mention this practicality before, provide some words of caution? For all the money I have paid him, never once did he point out the denial all of us have been trapped in. The focus has always been exclusively on Bart, without a thought or care to those of us Bart relies on in the day to day – or who relied upon Bart, once. The people – me – who are coping so badly with this new territory Bart has dragged us into.

Clarity.

Calm descends. A certainty solidifies in my bones. The sadness has not vanished. It has bonded to my cells, grafted to my DNA. Yet, there is peace in acceptance.

Exiting the house, my body lightens. I approach the gate. It is so easy. Buttons on the keypad are pressed in a minute. Another thirty seconds and an SMS with the new pass code flies through the cellular waves to Happiness. She is the only person, other than the therapist, who used it. Perhaps Dylan will be given it one day. But not this day.

Satisfaction spreads as I turn back to the house. I have dreamed of doing this for months. The fantasy would turn over and over as the should nots – the arguments, the explaining, the risks – mounted on top of one another. The weight of it all would press onto my lungs. It felt monumental.

Less than two minutes. That's all it took. A few buttons.

Done.

*

Noon approaches steadily forward. There are eggs to scramble, bread to slice and toast.

Another cup of tea.

Procrastination. It is the curse of the busy, or so says the myth. Those who need a reprieve from their heavy demands will put off a task in order to gain that breathing space. What else could possibly consume my time other than making lunch? Tea, apparently.

There are those who connect this behaviour with low self-esteem. To have low self-esteem, a person must have some. Do I hold myself in any esteem?

Then there is the theory that procrastination is a practice of avoidance created by stress. Tea is good for stress.

I inhale its aroma before each sip. It smells of sex. No wonder the English drink so much of it. Their secret inhibitions are toyed with while they press a cuppa directly under their nose. Rising to greet their nostrils is the essence of lightly fragranced oil smoothed onto musky bodies that surrender to one another under freshly laundered sheets. Hence the rosy complexions, I suppose.

Is this why I drink it in such large quantities as well? I do miss the smell of us, together, coupled, entangled with need. I long for much; look forward to little.

A sip.

Warmth spreads in my chest, easing the marbles, creating cracks where blood can now flow once again. I wait.

The gate bell rings.

Another sip.

The sense of certainty lingers. Dylan will not answer the gate.

The bell rings again.

Perhaps I am busy. Occupied, at the very least. Keeping watch as a security guard does, whose job is not of productivity, but to be at the ready. That is far from procrastination.

The bell rings a third time. A voice calls out. The hammock does not stir. To do nothing is as much of a decision as to do something. A sentiment I often forget.

A movement catches my eye. Dylan is near the compost bin, seemingly now deaf as he sorts the debris from his barrow.

My cell phone rings.

I fish it from my pocket; my suspicion of the caller's identity confirmed. The phone is switched off and promptly returned to where it came. I raise my cup to my lips as I keep sentry, waiting for Dylan to resume work at the front. He has become my signalman.

The tea has grown stale. The dregs are tossed into the sink. Tap turned on, mug placed under the stream. The water runs over my index finger, snaking its way along the web, working down my palm until the edge of my sleeve is damp. These clinging paths are made possible by surface tension, the water's skin, shivering and moving as one. It seems alive, and there is the odd dissenting scientist who will claim this is so.

Mug placed on draining board, wet palm brought up to my lips. A kiss.

A car door slams in the background.

I suppose my actions could be classified as being passive aggressive. Is that always wrong? Or is it simply practical to be realistic about one's chances in an all-out confrontation? The man hovering outside and I are like dry grains of sand. There is nothing to keep us together. As he has made clear, his relationship is with Bart and only Bart. I owe him nothing. Bart is welcome to seek him out, pay him, make the infinite cups of tea. Or not. Isn't that what the therapist has advised in all other matters? Bart's choice.

A car's engine ignites. It hovers, then drifts away to my left, comes back around, creeping up at my right. I freeze as the property is circled again and again, finally fading off to the left.

I wait and watch while the calm offers its support. Dylan tilts his head. Then, as if nothing at all has happened, he raises the wheelbarrow, his long legs striding forward.

And nothing has happened.

Yet it was something, all the same.

I step out onto the stoep. The midday breeze brushes against my cheek, toying with a tendril of hair. The mountaintops gleam under the November sun's radiance.

Now it is time to wake my husband. The three of us will have lunch together. Hopefully this arrangement will force us all to eat without protest or excuse.

It has been months since I have undertaken to wake Bart for lunch. There was a period where I did. It was like playing the slots. A press on his body could produce anything from anger, to a nod, to having him eat five bites of the meal with an expectation of applause. Then the day came where I reached out my hand and it began to tremble. I will not live in fear, I vowed. So he was left to his midday sleep, while I firmly refused to acknowledge that fear manifests itself in infinite forms. Like a shadow, fear follows as you run.

Today, calm accompanies me as I steadily extend the back of my hand. It brushes a shaven face, tracing the cheekbone as my fingers dip into the hollows. His head turns towards my touch. A curl skirts along my skin. His long eyelashes flutter, beautiful and thick, despite his body's wilt. Kai's were the same.

His hand comes up and meets mine. Palm to palm, pressing the back of my hand into his cheek. His eyes open. They are a liquid shimmer of sunlight brushed across the sea, after the sky is finished with its display of bright orange and pinks. Electric brandy, a colour I've only seen perfectly captured in glass.

That is not precisely true. Glass is actually a liquid that moves so slowly it isn't discernible to the eye. Most people forget that. Not Bart. Perhaps that is why he is so successful at getting glass to obey his will.

He blinks under my stare. His eyes used to convey emotion. Now they are virtually unreadable. Until his features animate, I cannot predict the temperament. I wait. The plain words originally planned no longer seem appropriate with his palm coupled with mine.

He lets out a sigh. Soft. They so often seem shaded with grey, but this one puffs out lined with white. A restful sleep, it says. Then the sides of his temples dip, crinkle and then …I no longer know what to expect.

'Are you disappointed in me?' he says.

His honesty is pleasing, the acknowledgment that his nap in the hammock was not an accident. But there is no equally honest answer I can offer in return. What could I say: Yes, but I understand it is because you have a disease? No, but nonetheless I am upset? Yes, why don't you fight? No, I am merely sad? I am whatever you want me to be, as long as it would help?

Each reply would leave me feeling cheap. This situation does not compact itself into a sound bite. The words refuse to form. The silence takes over, saying everything that needs to be said.

He presses my hand harder. There is a praying mantis perched near his head. What has brought them all out today? Weeks can go by without a single one showing itself. The creature bows. We have stooped so low that now the insect world is obliged to appeal on our behalf.

I lick my dry lips, attempt a smile. The skin stretches, pulls, a break. He extends his other arm, his thumb tracing my lip. He draws back. There is blood.

'You don't have to answer,' he says.

'I fired the therapist.'

The words stun. My mouth has become the noonday cannon on top of Signal Hill.

A smile pulls at his mouth.

'I'm not paying for him anymore,' I say.

The small smile remains. It does not grow bigger, nor does it diminish. Its genuine tilt, so reminiscent of times before, those shared secret looks we used to pass between us during his mother's boorish dos. My lungs clog while rocks rumble down my throat, piling up in my belly. My bladder aches with the weight.

'I'm not going to the meeting,' he says.

'I know.'

'You are upset.'

The smile is still there. I want to ask why. Is he happy that I am here, with the back of my hand pressed to his face? Or is he pleased to have frustrated us all in his refusal to play an active part in a business – a marriage! – that he helped create? But this smile is so precious I cannot bear to destroy it.

'It's no longer any of my business,' I say.

The praying mantis bows, rises again.

'But you fired him?'

'It was my money. That is my business.'

Still smiling. My breath ekes out through cracks between the stacked stones, which have piled so high that they press against the soft pallet. My bladder is urgent. His fingers tighten around my upturned palm. An ache settles into my wrist.

'You will find someone else.'

His voice states it as if there could be no other possibility, but it isn't something I had seriously considered. Do I possess the energy to sift through suitable candidates? To plead, cajole, demand that Bart go? Where would I find the strength to do this? He has used me up.

'Yes.' The word is said with such confidence, as if I had planned to say so all along. As if I possess self-esteem. As if Old Ella has planted both her feet beside this man.

A tiny nod. The smile still there. 'Maybe it was time.'

Another rock hurdles into my mouth. My jaw aches. The weight is too much. My bladder cannot bear it.

'I'll be back with lunch. Just now.'

He kisses my hand. His lips are dry. They scratch, making my skin tingle. I glance over at the insect. The praying mantis bobs, like a priest blessing our vows. I've made a commitment all over again.

So heavy.

My hand is released.

I flee. Fingers tingling. Wrist sore. Calm gone. The sobs escape the moment my naked skin touches the cool toilet seat. My stomach heaves, vomiting up the rocks, invisible to the naked eye. There is nothing there, yet everything. My bladder releases its burden with a gush. The tears I promised I would not shed refuse to cease. My tongue laps them off my cheeks as if it will return Kai to my womb.

But even Jesus Christ did not rise again as a baby boy.

Or so the story goes.

NOONTIDE

The shell cracks against the ceramic edge. The contents slide to the base of the bowl, yolk hovering in the albumen. I pluck out another from the pail. Its shell is almost the same shade as my fingernails. My thumb grazes the surface. To the pad's touch the egg is smooth; the microscopic holes are undetectable. They say there can be anywhere between 7,000 to 17,000 pores on a single eggshell. Who bothered to tally them? Does the poor sod, to this day, find himself counting egg pores in his sleep?

The second yolk slides down to quiver next to the first. This one has an orangeish hue, much like the sunrise. I crack another, and another, and another until half a dozen large button faces gleam up at me, shivering.

The oven beeps, announcing that its temperature is perfect. I abandon the bowl to slide a tray bearing thickly sliced bread under the grill. Our toaster cannot accommodate such girth. This method is far more time consuming, but what do I have to offer this earth but time? Besides, this method is supposed to be better, or so I read: a British chef bemoaning in an interview how the modern day electric toaster has ruined the art of toasting. I should locate that article and give it to Kamala. It would pair well with her thoughts on butter.

The fork pierces a yolk; there is always an initial resistance before the golden orb yields, bleeding into the albumen, finally consenting to mix with its neighbours. My wrist spins, the contents swirl, the colours spiralling around one another in increasingly smaller threads. A dash of milk and a pinch of seasoning, sending out tendrils. The milk is gradually absorbed, becoming part of the mix. The herbs, however, refuse to submit.

It is much like playing with opposing ends of a magnet, except with eggs there is a chance I'll win. I went through a phase, when I was very small, when I would sit for hours focused intently on trying to force the magnets to attach where they repelled. But then one day a busybody told my mother about a child who swallowed a handful of magnets. Their attracting forces twisted the intestines. The child died before the surgeon could cure. After that, my intriguing objects were locked away.

I would have allowed Kai to play with magnets. Even now.

I cannot decide what this says about me.

The mixture slops into the waiting pan with a collective squish, where it begins to softly sizz in the melted butter. Steam rises as I wait for it to set. This, according to Thad, is imperative to making scrambled eggs. He is as passionate on the subject as Kamala is about butter. Bart, in better days, once admitted to preparing scrambled eggs in the microwave.

'Stop talking,' Thad had said, 'before you ruin a beautiful friendship.'

I wonder if, after all of this, they can still be considered friends? If Bart does ever get better, will the two men pick up where they left off? Or will they have to feel it out, much like first dates?

I suppose that question applies to all of us treading in Bart's wake. Even me.

Especially me.

A pop from the pan attracts my attention. The mixture is starting to gel. This, according to Thad, is when one begins a series of slow figure eights. I can't recall his particular objection to a fast scramble. But the languid pace does have a rather soothing rhythm. The mind is allowed to wander, dream up journeys for the steam created by the paring of egg to heat.

Eggs are seventy-four percent water. I use the borehole supply for the garden and the chickens. The chickens are fed scraps from my own vegetable patch. Thus, the feathered beasts are composed of the very same plants that thrive on the chicken's composted excrement and the ashes of my son. We are all interlinked.

The steam coats my hand and brushes my cheeks. I imagine they are pieces of my son's soul. Perhaps they are. Perhaps he is, at this moment, drifting upwards from my pan, essence of him captured in the makeup of H_2O, now liberated.

My eyelids shut. For a moment his face comes into perfect focus. Yet he is still too far to touch.

The sound of shuffling footsteps flings my eyes wide open. Irritation coats me. A familiar voice, 'Do you need help?'

My shoulders hunch protectively over the eggs, my hand's grip on the pan becomes fierce and possessive. I shoot a glance over at Bart, curls in disarray, looking dramatically taller, like a new shoot of bamboo. Emotions morph into confusion as my brain grapples with this stretched out man. He blinks. My lids flutter in reply. Then clarity: this is my husband standing up straight; the long-stooped shoulders pushed back, head no longer bowed.

My body uncoils. 'You could check on the toast in the oven. It may be ready to turn.' The words come out casually, defying my shock.

Bart opens the oven door without comment.

The spatula barely moves as I watch in a mystified awe. Steadily, he slides out the tray.

Old Bart would have asked why I was making toast in the oven, rather than in our perfectly adequate toaster. Old Bart would have teased, even after I drummed out my practical defence. Now this New Ella is too stunned by New Bart's most meagre offer of willing assistance to inquire what has inspired such events to unfold, with shoulders back.

Unselfconsciously, he examines the bread before flipping the slices with his bare hands. It seems these new soft fingers, though devoid of calluses, mysteriously retain their imperviousness to heat.

I hastily return to the eggs, dismayed to see they are now clutching the pan's surface.

'Anything else I can do?'

I almost choke. Old Ella would have seized this moment and let go, unleashing all that Bart *could* do. Yet, I hear myself say, 'Perhaps you could set the table. For three, please.' The words are still calm, casual, giving no indication of how much effort it takes to act so natural. This hurts. We used to be this moment every day, a duet of give and take. We were a team, working through the array of household chores and the mundane details that litter modern lives.

His mother thought me an awful wife for not tending to my husband's every need. She once accused me of being weak. 'I never required my husband to help me with my domestic duties,' she said, conveniently overlooking the whole army of underpaid staff she employed.

How odd that after she passed, I melted into the daughter-in-law she'd pined for. Would she prefer this Ella? Or would she be delighting in my downfall? Perhaps she does, from wherever it is she now dwells.

Muscles tighten; another marble added to the collection. It is impossible to decide if this is his idea of an apology or his warped way of rewarding me for not forcing him to attend the meeting. Perhaps a moment of gloom has lifted now that we seem to have acquired a brief understanding over the matter of therapy. What is painfully absent, however, is the sensation of hope. There is only suspicion, with a touch of anger lurking deep. Don't fuck with me, I want to growl.

My mind casts back to this morning, when he noted the day of the week. How much of his depression is real? How much of it is a manipulative act? Because these moments are not unheard of, simply rare, the periods between them growing the longer we plough on. Never once have they led on to better times.

His hand slips by my hip, brushing the pelvic bone. I glance down, noticing how desperately the denim hangs from jutting bones, as if begging for a belt.

'Pardon,' he says, gently pulling open the drawer that holds the silver.

'Set for three, please,' I say.

The hairs on his arms tickle my exposed flesh along the waistband of my jeans. I glance up. Over his shoulder, the clock on the wall insists that it is only a quarter past noon.

How can it be so early?

I focus on the minute hand, ticking by at the usual speed. I feel another soft brush. The tink-tink of the silver reaches my ears. I wait for the clock to slow, to fall in line with this moment, but obliviously, it trots. I've become trapped behind an invisible film, condemned to look upon a world where time steadily proceeds, while my body and mind are caught in an endless loop. It is the same arguments, the same mind tricks, the same food, the same chores, the same frustrations day in and day out. We begin again, but make no progress.

He draws back, the soft hair abandoning my flesh. His dry lips brush my temple. The silver catches the light, shooting a shard into my eye. I refuse to wince. It would be misinterpreted as a rejection of his touch. We've been here before, an innocent instinctive reaction of mine unleashing a raid of anger. There are hydrangeas everywhere; some are simply in disguise.

Someday that hydrangea will die.

He flicks his elbow against the drawer and walks off. The silver winks as it is whisked back into the darkness. If it were not for Happiness, they would be a tarnished mess. But the woman is determined to keep them at a perfect shine.

My mother-in-law would be so pleased. It was she who began the tradition of using them for everyday. 'Might as well enjoy it now before it gets stolen. Nothing lasts long in this country.'

After she died I decided that it was time to acquire basic flatware, easy to clean and less pretentious.

'What a waste of money,' Bart had said. 'How bourgeois to need more of what we've already got. Do you think Happiness cares if she is polishing silver or cleaning the windows?'

As it happened, Happiness did care. 'I like having an excuse to sit while I work.'

I had been so embarrassed. 'Do you need more breaks? Please, rest more if you need.'

The look she shot me made it clear she'd thought I'd gone barking mad. But all she said was, 'Can I make you a cup of tea?'

Every day I give thanks that the teacups and mugs are all mine. It was a gradual project, a bit like the hydrangea will be, I suspect.

The china, however, is progressing slower than the mugs. Ringed with prancing ponies, I detest these obscenely whimsical, loathsomely functional objects. Yet, this is all I have to serve lunch on. Jabbing the spatula into the pan, I pry out the dried-out mess, dumping it on the plates. By my calculations it will be another year or so until only the odd saucer and bowl remain and my desire to replace them will be considered practical.

I suppose my strategy is passive aggressive. Or perhaps it is passive resistance. Because if the therapist's theories on Bart's depression are correct, then the disagreements over the hydrangea, the silver, and china are not actually with Bart. I am arguing with depression. As a something that is not actually a thing in the most tangible sense, there is no sword to best it. It is this illusive whisper that hinders battle with rationale.

Or I am merely rationalising. Sounds rather pathetic. But the promise to marry Bart was to Bart and only Bart; not a third party, not a creature that has sunk its fangs deep into my husband's soul and cares nothing for me. Depression is his ghoul, not mine. Yet, I know that I will not crack a single plate today. Pick your battles, they say. Wise advice.

*

Dylan cuts his food into perfectly formed pieces. Each bite is chewed with deliberate, yet unhurried intent. He keeps his expression neutral, despite my suspicion that the man is incredibly ill at ease eating lunch with us. Bart, however, is masticating (disgusting word, but the right one for such action) with such careless force that he might as well just come out and say it: You overcooked the eggs.

I know, I want to say in return. Instead I sip my tea, wishing it was wine. Somehow we seem to have all agreed not to talk. Probably for the best. Perhaps I shouldn't have had us eat together. Then again, everyone is eating. That is something.

An excruciatingly awkward something.

Have the two men even introduced themselves to one another? I look at them both and consider breaking the silence, but then stop myself. Why should I? They've had plenty of opportunity this morning to exchange names.

Still, I wonder. Something about the way Dylan sits here at the table makes it seem that he simply accepts Bart as part of the property, like the hydrangea out front. And Bart? Perhaps Bart accepts Dylan's presence strictly because he cannot be bothered to do otherwise. It would require effort, an amount of caring of what is happening outside his own self-centred existence. And the only thing happening is that my husband can hardly swallow his over-dried eggs.

They are revolting.

Dylan, of course, would not and will not comment on the dehydrated state of his lunch. He who requires nothing but food, in whichever form I wish to present it. A man who will not tell me if he prefers an egg fried, boiled or poached, is simply pleased to be able to consume it. Who plucks a linen serviette from his lap and dabs his mouth before relaying the cloth with such care it is devoid of wrinkles. Who is eating with such a well-mannered hand it would make many a headmistress weep with joy.

I want to shake him and say, why are you doing this to yourself? You are clearly well educated, and were offered a job with far more hours and yet you are here.

He'd already been to hell. That's what he told Luxolo. I've heard the stories. I can only imagine. Yet, I cannot help wondering if a woman with a suckling baby, whose milk threatened to dry up without more food, would be able to turn down such an opportunity no matter what terrible memories it may bring?

I jab a forkful of egg into my mouth, as shame creeps over me. What possesses me to even begin to debate Dylan's choices while I'm sitting pretty on my trust fund, feeling overwhelmed that I have to help my husband wash?

Although, if I had no money and a desperate baby, I'd have walked out on Bart while he rotted. At least I would like to believe that I would have. But that does not excuse the fact that here I am, sitting comfortably in a chair on my stoep, eating overcooked eggs served on a china plate, stabbing them with a silver fork, while looking out onto a view of mountains, often wishing there was at least a strip of sea visible. Privileged. Miserable.

I swallow hard, trying to push down my internal embarrassment, which is threatening to reveal itself as hot red cheeks. I am ridiculous. Possibly in as much need of a medical pick-me-up as my mental abyss of a husband.

Although I suppose then one must begin to debate if I am merely grieving or depressed. I always supposed grief, unlike depression, must be allowed, like an open wound, to heal on its own. That the drugs were a plaster, stifling, holding the infection in and impeding the mending process. Where depression can be partly due to a chemical imbalance. Depression is a place beyond grief, a disease that could have invaded regardless of Kai, his death a mere trigger. Or am I wrong again? Do I need a pill as badly as my husband?

It's not that Bart should be happy. Or that medication would make it so. I'm not happy. In rather a short span of time I have lost my son, a mother-in-law and, in many ways, my husband. That isn't a chemical imbalance; it is a miserable existence. A misery that has sprung from very real loss. People should be entitled to time to work through grief. Grief should not have to hide behind fake smiles, platitudes and pills.

I have a glass of wine every night.

For now, that is enough.

Bart hardly drinks. An occasional beer or the odd glass of wine and the man is done. Which is odd, all things considered. But perhaps a pill could at least nudge him towards trying. To face the fact that there is a future and must be lived. But he won't consider it. Maybe this will change when I find a new therapist.

My husband shoves back his chair, the metal screeching against the paving. He stands up and with barely a nod in my direction, he departs. His plate and cup remain, neither finished.

Dylan lifts his mug while keeping his gaze pointedly towards the peaks.

I glance down at my plate. My stomach rolls, no longer able to tolerate the disgust with myself, Bart and the ghastly meal. Yet I cannot bear tossing out this food. Not today, not while Dylan sits next to me.

'Think of all the starving children in Africa,' my headmistress would often say.

'I'm from Africa,' I once replied.

'Think of the dark ones, then,' she had said.

I am fairly certain she is now retired. Probably for the best.

Dylan and I wordlessly work through the remaining meal. He, with the same poise as he began. I, now masticating, swallowing hard, trying to give off an air of being fine. Content. As I should be, having been spared the agony of living in a constant state of not-enough-to-eat. But the bites become smaller and smaller. A burning sensation joins the nausea in my stomach. I look down at my food in dismay.

'May I take your plate, ma'am?' Dylan says.

I glance over and see he is now standing, his plate and Bart's already in hand. My stomach leaps into my throat, threatening to upend its contents if I say no. 'It's Ella, and yes. Thank you. Very kind.'

'A pleasure, ma'am,' he says, adding the plate to the pile. My stomach weeps in gratitude, as the burning nausea battles to contain itself. But as he walks off the remaining eggs on my plate jiggle and taunt. Guilt settles into my lap.

I sit in solitude, trying to cool my distressed digestive track. There is now a different quiet than the one we shared at lunch. This one is less lonely. Which makes no sense logically, but is true.

My belly lets out an odd yowl as two hadedas coast into the garden with an ear-piercing caw. I imagine ants on the ground scattering as the birds brace for a landing. They flutter their feathers, before tucking in their wings neatly. The sunlight catches their iridescent sides as they peruse their surroundings, proceeding to plunge long beaks into the earth.

I tilt my head, feeling tension uncoil. A gentle warmth spreads. A sense of pleasure, a soft delight. I've always carried a certain fondness for this mini pterodactyl-like creature. If reincarnation were possible, I would not mind returning as one. They tend to travel in groups of twos or threes. Companionship without the stifling existence of being part of a school, pack or flock.

Most people I've encountered dislike the hadeda's call, which does bear a certain resemblance to an air-raid warning siren. Perhaps it is. They fly like children on their first pair of rollerskates.

'Watch out, here I come,' they bellow, flaying away as they propel themselves forward, unsure of how they will stop. I appreciate this frank announcement. It is honest and without apology. 'We're trying,' their graceless flight seems to say. 'What more could we possibly do?'

My stomach gives a startling flop, briefly lurching upwards. I normally avoid naps. Bart behaviour. But in this particular instance a lie-down may be necessary. The hammock is empty. No doubt my husband has installed himself in bed. It is this habit of constant slumber that has motivated Happiness to launder the sheets twice a week. Such a waste of water and work.

I get up and carefully make my way to the hammock, disrupting the birds. They waddle with as much awkwardness as they fly. By the time I've reached the hammock, however, they've returned to their methodical pecking. I've heard that their search for food helps aerate the lawn, but that their excrement may kill the grass. I suspect the latter is nothing more than a vicious rumour spread by the hadeda-haters.

I tumble into the tasselled canvass, which readily accepts my weight. It smells of Bart. Not the sour odour that brings to mind his mental and physical decay. But that scent that is simply his, lurking underneath any other smell, be it soap or sweat, imprinted on my memory. I take a deep breath, filling my lungs with Bart-ness. The burn in my belly subsides. Second-hand comfort. It doesn't last, this aromatic equivalent of a fingerprint. Both the mind and the nose forget and eventually the scent fades. I tried to preserve the essence of Kai, refusing to allow his beloved blanket to be washed. Perhaps I smelled it all up. But it is gone, sitting just beyond the reach of my olfaction recollection. Sometimes it teases my brain, as if I let my nostrils drift through the air currents at the perfect angle, then I could capture that sweetness again. To remember that soft, wonderful smell that was my boy. So close. It was the perfect scent.

The hammock rocks gently. My gut groans, then settles, the burn almost squelched. This is a good hammock. Perhaps not in the way of a wicker basket, which apparently conveys glowing health. But hammocks do crop up in advertisements, proclaiming peace and calm. Tranquillity. The sturdy canvas holds the body in a way that eases aches. When one is swinging in the breeze, life drifts by in a manner completely different than when one is sitting upright. Maybe this is why Bart is so fond of it these days.

My finger slips over a tassel. The bobbles are softer than the day we bought it. A purchase spurred by Bart's enthusiasm. When he pulled me into the shop I was sceptical. I wondered if the attraction was due to what this object seemed to promise rather than what it could actually provide. I had visions of it mouldering under the trees, a symbol of unattainable relaxation.

'Is this an anti-capitalist argument?' he had asked.

'That isn't really my point,' I had said.

He put his hand on its rail and climbed in. 'Ah, this is very nice. But go on, explain your point.'

I'd looked at him, so content, and felt rather ashamed of my reluctance. 'It's that we are so busy. When would we use this?'

He reached out, beckoning. 'Come, lie next to me.'

I'd accepted his hand and, with the help of the shop assistant, joined in.

'Isn't this nice?' His fingers ran through my hair, my head fitted perfectly on that space between shoulder and chest.

'It is nice,' I had said.

'But?'

'I don't want it to mock me.'

He let out a soft laugh. 'Mock you? How would it mock you?'

'I don't want it hanging there, swinging in the breeze, reminding me that I've forgotten how to chill.'

'Ah.' He kissed the side of my head. 'So what you are saying is that we don't stop and smell the roses anymore.'

'That's such a cliché.'

'But one with a point.'

The shop assistant, lurking outside my line of vision, gave the hammock a gentle push. As it rocked, I realised I was a goner. It felt so good.

'We're getting it,' Bart said into my ear.

I drew my eyebrows in.

'Yes,' he said. 'And my personal mission will be to see that you use it.'

'You mean, that you will use it.'

'No,' he said, tweaking my nose. 'I know I will, but I'm going to make sure you do, too.'

He was true to his promise. He'd catch my hand as I was darting around and lead me to the hammock. I found myself using it more and more, even when he wasn't around. I loved it when I was pregnant. Later it became the perfect place to nurse Kai. In fact, it isn't until recently that I've shunned it. Which is odd, given that this is truly the first time in my adult life where I've had plenty of time to lie around. It has become Bart's place.

I run my foot along the rail. The hammock shifts at the movement. Kai may have been conceived in this. An event that might sound terribly romantic and was actually rubbish. Yet... not.

We were both lying here, together, cocooned under the stars not saying much. This is what I used to love about being married, how we could happily exist in quiet companionship. Now it is awful, this silence. But then it was bliss, to be there doing nothing, his body heat melding with mine, the sounds of the night. He was right when we purchased the hammock; we had needed a place to have moments of shared peace. But that night the calm companionship evolved, as these things often do: a nuzzle on the neck, a finger straying over sensitive skin.

Sex in a hammock, however, is not like sex in the back of a car, against a shower wall, or on a countertop. In fact, for it to work, I suppose we should have treated it more like a countertop. Bart could have found his purchase on the ground, me sitting sideways rather than lying in it the traditional manner, I guess. But it never occurred to either of us at the time.

Instead we were rather squashed and any attempted movement brought to mind a fish flopping on dry land. I couldn't help it; I laughed. It was all so terribly ridiculous and hopeless. Then he began to laugh as well, until we were both laughing directly into each other's mouths, echoing laughter, still craving that release sex brings. We couldn't stop, despite it being lousy. Eventually the hammock gave up on us, tossing us to the ground, where we proceeded to get on with it well enough.

How is it that a child conceived in laughter could be doomed to such a tragic life? Perhaps the calendar lied and this was not the time Kai began to be. But given everything that happened that month, it always did seem the most likely. Is that why Bart favours the hammock? Does he remember our awkward attempt at being spontaneously original? Probably not. Maybe he remembers the shop. The promise of peace, waiting for it to come and ease the haunting memories of the cell phone. Or perhaps he simply stews in guilt.

And why do I keep analysing any of this?

Let go.

I can't.

*

My cell rings. I thrust my hand into my pocket, tilting the hammock. I throw out an arm for balance, still fumbling for the phone. Righting myself, the hammock begins to rock back and forth as I bring the screen to view: Kamala.

'Hello,' I say. My voice sounds as dry as the scrambled eggs.

'Hello,' she says. 'Thad told me that every person is allowed two hours to wallow. Your time is up.'

I let out a soft snort. 'Where did he get that?'

'I have no idea. Don't even try to look it up on the internet. It's probably some Greek thing.'

'Greek thing? Thad cannot possibly try to defend his position on wallowing on the basis of it being Greek. They can be a terribly morose lot.'

'Mykonos is morose? The Greek Islands are infamous for their partying.'

'Kamala, one of their most revered philosophers drank hemlock.'

'Socrates was executed!'

'His friends tried to rescue him yet he refused to leave prison.'

'Ella, the man was making a profound political point.'

'He was an egotistical depressive that had a temper tantrum of fatal proportions.'

There is a pause before she says, 'Are we discussing Socrates or Bart?'

I scratch my thigh and gaze upward, feeling rather bereft at how the conversation has evolved. For a brief moment I felt like myself, not Old Ella, but a me-of-now, coping and talking like a regular person balancing her wounds with humour and the positives of life: food, shelter, a garden, a gardener, running water, Happiness, a living husband. . .

'Fine,' she says, 'we're changing the subject. What are you doing?'

Licking my dry cracked lips, I consider lying. But such action is a bit too much like an alcoholic claiming to have only a single glass while hiding the empty bottles in the bottom of gumboots and in the rafters.

'Ella? Hello? Starting to worry me. What are you doing?'

I flick a fly on the rail. It zips into the air, making complicated patterns. 'I am lying down in the hammock.'

'You are wallowing,' she says.

'I am not wallowing, I am simply trying to recover from a severe case of indigestion.'

'How did you get indigestion? Your stomach was perfectly fine after eating my croissants.'

I glance down at my belly. My protruding hipbones glare back accusingly. 'Because, my pesky and irritating friend, I overcooked the scrambled eggs.'

'How on earth did you manage to screw that up?'

'Bart was trying to help.'

'Oh. Oh my.

'Quite.'

She pauses.

I tug a strand of hair into view and study the split ends, as I was prone to do at boarding school.

She says, 'Do you want to talk about it?'

'No.'

A dragonfly begins to buzz near a large avocado leaf. Avo leaves would be an excellent substitute for toilet paper, should the need arise. Mango leaves often have a rippled edge and that could be problematic. But the slim smooth build of the avo causes me to question the entire design of toilet paper. How did toilet paper's width get decided? Was it something to do with the machine making it, or did somebody do a study on the ideal dimensions?

'Fine,' Kamala says. Her earlier cheery tone has vanished. 'We can talk about something else. But I'm not letting you hang up until you talk to me and I am reassured you are not going to spend the rest of the day being miserable.'

I am always miserable, I think. 'I am going to get up. Soon, in fact.'

'Maybe I should come by. We can have tea.'

'That would be lovely, but no. I have to start editing your photos and I am meeting Luxolo at three.'

'What's he want?' Her voice is snappish, ready to leap to my defence.

I love you, I think. 'He doesn't want anything. He is helping me.'

'Another swimming lesson?'

I gnaw on the edge of my lip; dry skin slipping into the space between my teeth, floss of the cannibals. 'Actually, no. Not exactly.'

'Ella?'

Awkwardness nudges my shoulders and they hunch near my ears in reply. 'We're going scuba diving.'

'What?'

I shut my eyes. This was never supposed to be a secret, but I suppose nobody other than Luxolo and I know. Private. Personal. There should be a difference between these things and the shame of the hush-hush.

'Ella, when did this happen? Are you actually going into the sea?'

'Um, it appears to be so.'

'It appears to be so. Hey, what's going on?'

A marble begins to form, reigniting the queasy sensation in my stomach. 'He thought…no, it was more that…I was swimming, you see, with my head down and it seemed that perhaps…' Spit lodges in the back of my throat, making it impossible to continue. I try to clear it, releasing a repulsive little croak. I try again, wondering if Kamala thinks I've hung up. 'Sorry,' I say. 'Think I need water.'

'Well, that's one way to get you out of the hammock.'

'I wasn't trying to keep it a secret. I was simply, trying. Sorry, not being very clear.'

'You want to be brave. A stepping stone.'

The right words. 'Yes. A bit. I mean, I do not envision this becoming a new hobby.'

'I'm so proud of you,' she says.

A huge balloon of air is released from my lungs. The marble floating away, as if attached to it by string. Her voice is true, no underlying guilt or prodding – why didn't you tell me? 'Thank you,' I say.

'Have you practiced in the pool?'

'Yes.'

'A lot?'

'Yes. It has reached a point where even I think he is being overly cautious.'

'Well, with everything...'

'Yes, I know. And today is going to be a very short dive, just off the docks. Nothing fancy. Probably won't see a thing.'

'Still, wow. You must call me when it is done.'

'Yes, okay,' I say. I'm not sure I will. Perhaps I have to. For Kamala. So hard to communicate to anyone, though, after I have had my head submerged under water.

'Or you can leave it until tomorrow, if that's better,' she says.

'I love you.' The words shock me. I don't say such things out loud.

'I love you, too, Ella.'

I bite my lip.

'Ella?'

'Yes?'

'What's it like, breathing underwater?'

I think of the water coating me, my attempts to stay calm as my eyes blink in the bending light. How it feels as if I am touching him, yet arguing with his killer. 'Loud,' I say.

'Loud?'

'Yes, it is rather loud. I had not anticipated that.'

'Like a Darth Vader mask?'

'A bit, but one that is attached to a hosepipe. Those bubbles are right in your ear as if you jumped into a fish tank.'

'I suppose that makes sense. I've always imagined it would be quiet.'

'I did, too.'

'Peaceful.'

I glance up into the green canopy of leaves. 'There is this feeling of solitude.'

'Like at a really loud party and it's as if you can hide under the noise?'

'Yes, a bit.' More like giving birth, I think. All those people around, yet when the pushing begins, it all comes down to you.

Alone.

*

'What's your greatest fear?' Luxolo had asked, the other week.

It's already happened, I'd thought. But such retorts are not suitable while out in public, if ever. We were tucked in a corner of the local pool, trying to keep our distance from the elderly holidaymakers and the scattering of mothers with babies. Even so, we were in public. 'Are you asking in the general sense, or something specific?'

'Scuba diving,' he said.

'Drowning.'

He reached out and tenderly tucked an errant lock of mine behind my ear. 'Yes, I know. But I need specifics; what is it you think will go wrong?'

I glanced down at the water and studied the flotsam. Flotsam: a disgusting word, much like masticate, and which should typically be used in reference to debris in the ocean. But to see the skin flakes, the scabs, the hair, the fingernail clippings, the creamy streams that I suspect are cum, all twisting in the sunlit water—flotsam is the only word that truly represents my disgust. Occasionally I'll try to tell myself it is plankton and pretend we are in the sea, but the lie rarely works. After each session I immediately shower in the changing rooms, having another as soon as I am home, soaping my hair twice. It is a minor mercy that I've not become ill.

'Ella,' he said, lowering his face into view. 'Talk to me. We need to discuss your fears so I can address them.'

I turned slightly away. It is difficult to explain the myriad nightmares that plague both when I am asleep and awake. The one where I stand witness to my son's death: the chubby arms waving, the pink feet kicking helplessly as the mouth opens and closes with no sound until his body begins to convulse. I am always frozen. An inner voice will scream, beg, plead for my arms to reach out and pick up my boy, to lift his sweet body and pull him tight to my chest.

Then there is the one where I have shrunk and found myself dwelling inside him. Looking upwards, I watch the water thrust itself though his nasal cavity, down the trachea, raining upon my head. In the end we drown together. I am caught in his water-filled lungs. I fear the burn, the bursting need for breath, the urgency with no way of release, where every second can feel like an agonising hour and actual death can take minutes upon minutes. Of all the ways to die, it seems one of the cruellest. And none of this is something I'll speak about in public.

Luxolo gently, firmly, gripped my arms and turned me to face him. But I had refused to meet his gaze. 'Okay, Ella, listen to me. Don't freeze up. Next week it's just off the docks. It isn't going to be deep. So the normal problems – lack of oxygen in the tank, the bends, or whatever is going through your head – are not an issue. We'll be just below the surface, exactly like it is in the pool. And at any moment, we can pop right up into that sweet, sweet air.'

'It's the regulator,' I said, finally looking him in the eye. It is the truth, and perfectly fine to admit out in the open. 'I keeping fretting about it getting knocked out. I tense up every time we practice.'

'Right. Then we'll suit up and go over it again. But remember, next week, as long as you don't panic, if it gets knocked out and you're feeling funny about it, then just give me the thumbs up and we're up. I'm gonna be holding your hand.'

The sweep is graceful, a ballerina moving her arms from second position to first, which catches the line holding the regulator, bringing it against the body. I tell myself to remain calm while keeping my focus on the light playing off the water, the way it bends and moves in fishnet patterns, warped by the water molecules. I've captured the regulator first try, every time. But then there is purging of the mouthpiece, exhaling sharply or two bursts from the valve. Screw this up and the person inhales water.

'It's not gonna happen,' Luxolo tells me each time I bring this up. 'You do what you're supposed to do and there is nothing to worry about.'

Every time we go through the drill the fear is there, lurking, that I haven't done it correctly. A split second before I inhale, the doubt shoots through with a sharp painful force. This is it, I always think.

We practiced the manoeuvre again and again. Calmness eventually settled in my limbs. The fear turned to acceptance. We all have to die at some point, why not today, I'd reasoned. At least I can say I tried, for whatever that's worth.

What is anything worth?

But I did. Try. And afterwards, in the parking lot, my friend gave me a kiss on the cheek. 'Go well,' he said.

To go well, I must have been well at some point.

We do act like I am well. On the drive home that day, I realised that Luxolo has never brought up my husband when we are face to face. We act like life is fine, minus my issues with putting my head underwater. I am a normal human being around Luxolo, or at least he treats me as if I am one. Unless I mention Bart. Even then, I keep those comments limited to a brief vent. Otherwise all business pertaining to Bart – meetings not attended, bills needing to be paid – are all conducted over the phone, where I am permitted to be less normal.

Nor can I recall Luxolo ever bringing up Kai. The closest he came was at the reception, 'I have no words to express the depth of your loss.'

I do, I had thought. Hell. I am spiralling down Dante's rings while everyone offers, 'My deepest sympathies. Please do not hesitative to let me know if there is anything I can do.'

You can't, I had thought. My son is already dead. But all I would say was, 'Thank you. You're so kind.'

Then the next thoughtful soul would shove yet another sickly sweetened cup of tea into my trembling hands. I've never taken sugar before or since.

Tea.

I need a cup.

I've yet to emerge from the hammock. My tongue has become thick with cotton wool. This really won't do. Far too Bart-ish. With that dreadful thought, I swing my legs over the side. Blood rushes down, my vision tunnels, the garden spins. Definitely require more tea. I breathe carefully. My vision begins to clear. Kamala says she gets head-rushes too. Says they have worsened since she became pregnant.

It is good that she phoned. Not like a wicker basket, but the goodness of the actual organic vegetables whose worth is not tangible to the eye. A carrot is a carrot regardless of how it is grown, but the taste, the nutritional content, the effects on the body long after it is consumed are not the same. Her phone call cannot be packaged or quantified.

Her words hold me into the now, the actual day that demands

to be lived. Yet I cannot help but notice that she too, leaves words out, questions unasked. She did not inquire if I remain afraid of putting my head into the water, if I dread going with Luxolo at three. Perhaps she was worried her question would make the fear more real. It is good that she remains my friend despite me having become what I now am, despite everything.

Jama and Dumisani, however, can no longer be considered friends. They have left their rants, the negotiations, their concerns about the business to be fed through Luxolo. There have always been invisible lines dictating our relationship. For them, I was always Bart's wife. This is different to my relationship with Luxolo, who views me as Ella, who happens to be married to his partner, Bart. Jama and Dumisani were friends with Bart, as businessmen, as artists, as brothers of water. I suppose with Bart no longer participating in any of those activities there is nothing left of their relationship.

Friendships, relationships, they have all begun to feel carefully categorised. Jama and Dumisani are furious with Bart, do not seem to have the first clue how to deal with *this* Bart (do any of us?), yet deep down I sense their loyalty would return if Bart were to re-engage. I suppose Kamala and Thad are my Jama and Dumisani. Thad was friends with Bart, but always through me. Bart: husband of Ella. I suppose this is how the friendships would divide in the event of a divorce.

Divorce.

The word hangs in the air, lingering, written in ornate script. Fancy calligraphy begins to decorate the D, weaving a design until it resembles the grand trellises adorning pretentious security gates. Open me, it says.

I try to swallow, but my dry throat rebels. With a scratchy sigh, I heave myself to my feet, the hanging word dispersing into the air. I need tea. My feet, however, insist on a stroll through the garden, the real garden, where my baby chards wave their tiny leaves attached to multi-coloured stems, the asparagus twists and coils until it will eventually become a feathery mess and the beetroots have begun to crest above the soil. This year I've added a row of Chioggia, the candy-striped beet, whose white and red markings amuse. I am sure Kamala and Thad will share my joy in these old-fashioned relics just as they did when I planted purple carrots. My stab at strawberry popcorn, however, will go down in gardening infamy. They say it is easy to grow.

'Hello, ma'am.'

My insides jump, but I force my body to calmly turn towards Dylan. His face looks composed, no sign of a smirk or merriment. I do not believe he intended to startle. 'Hello,' I say.

'Is there anything I can do here, ma'am?'

I glance around. There is always more work to be done: mulching, weeding, trimming, spraying leaves with diluted dish soap, scattering coffee grounds, pinching off pests, tying back, watering the seedlings which require more frequent intervals than the older plants which have their needs addressed via the automatic sprinklers. A gardener's job is never done. But I am not ready to share them yet.

'Thank you. Perhaps next week. I was out here most of yesterday, you see.'

'I understand, ma'am,' he says.

I don't believe you, I think.

He remains.

I wait.

So does he. There is a tickling along my forehead that there is something more he is expecting. I cast back to this morning, what we have said, how he came to be here, standing in front of me looking patient but with no sign of departing.

This whole experience is unlike the day I hired Happiness, who arrived at an appointed time and date with a lady who worked for Kamala. The lady introduced Happiness. I invited them in to chat over tea. After we sat down, I outlined my needs while Happiness laid out her expectations of pay and hours. We both consulted our diaries and arrived on two days that suited us both. It was all very civilised. Contracts ensued and then my nightmare dealings with the people at UIF began. But that has all, thankfully, been resolved.

Oh heavens, I will have to deal with that agency all over again for

Dylan.

'I haven't paid you,' I say.

'No ma'am, it is not the end of the day.'

'But we should discuss it.'

'You pay what you feel I am worth,' he says. 'That is all I require.'

Panic grips me. Oh no. This is not how it can be resolved. Sleep will elude me for his entire employment if his wage depends on my belief of his worth. The job he performs? Or his presence? Or who he is as a human being? What we are worth cannot be reflected in money or I would buy my son back immediately.

'I'm going to make a cup of tea.' It comes out as a croak.

'That's fine, ma'am.'

'No.' I motion with my hand. 'Come. Coffee.'

The vocal cords shrivel.

Inside, I immediately turn on the tap, filling two glasses with water. Thrusting one into Dylan's hands, I bring my own to my lips. The liquid flows down my throat, coating my tongue, running across my gums, the spaces between my teeth. My stomach accepts the water, allowing the cool to spread along my gut.

Lowering the depleted glass I see that he has not touched a single drop.

'Ma'am, I am in need of the washroom.'

I blink.

He sets his glass down. 'The lavatory, ma'am?'

'Yes,' I say, 'of course. I am so sorry. I should have shown you earlier.' My feet remain where they are.

'It's fine, ma'am.'

No, it isn't. Because until now he has probably been using the garden tap of unfiltered borehole water for a drink and been forced to relieve himself in a corner by a shrub. He should have been shown this basic facility upon being admitted to the property. But he was not, and now he is here, and I must show him to the toilet.

I take a step and stop. With three toilets in the house itself, plus the one in the granny flat, it should be a simple matter. But there is no clear answer to his most basic of questions. I cannot lead him to the en suite, it would require tip-toeing past Bart. Worse, we could walk in and find Bart himself, enthroned. The man never bothers to shut the door.

Nor would it be fair to ask Dylan to use the one in my office, which back in the day was originally used as the maid's quarters. There are storage sheds with more space, and like a shed, must be entered from the outside. Nor is there any privacy. The toilet is out in the open, directly next to a basic shower concealed by a cheap plastic curtain. There isn't even a sink, due to lack of space. On the odd occasion that I've made use of it, I've had to wash my hands using the dribbling showerhead. The whole situation is ridiculous. At the very least, I should have invested in one of those Japanese screens, but since my mother-in-law's passing I keep toying with relocating to the granny flat. The right time for such a move has yet to come.

Happiness does use the toilet in the granny flat, carved out of the original coach shed. She relocks the unit after each use. I suppose it is rather out of the way. However, she says she finds the shattered porcelain tub of the hall bathroom disturbing. I understand. But to require the man to go outside at this point would be insulting. Yet I cannot explain the tub. Nor do I have any idea when it was last used. There is a distinct probability the plumbing no longer works.

I take another step then pause. There is nothing to be done. The situation is what it is.

'Ma'am?'

'Sorry, terribly sorry. I'm afraid you'll have to excuse us.' My stride lengthens, the words rushing out. 'The hall bathroom is a work-in-progress; a bit of a mess.'

'I'm sure it is fine, ma'am,' he says.

He has no idea. Who would? I stop with sudden jerk. My hand motions to the door that I cannot bring myself to touch. 'Please, let me know if there is a problem. And do shut the door when you have finished.'

'Of course, ma'am.'

'Ella,' I say, before marching myself back into the kitchen.

The tap is thrust on with too much force, water sprays off the top of the kettle catching me in the face. I jump back, water from the kettle sloshing over my wrist.

'Bugger,' I say, plucking a tea towel from the sideboard.

I cannot remember how we got home after Bart was ushered outside the restaurant. Perhaps I had phoned Kamala and Thad. It seems like the sort of thing I would do. I simply remember our home being filled with strangers – paramedics? Police? The therapist, definitely. By my mother-in-law's request. He gave her an injection. I know this because I've been told the story, repeatedly, by the very man himself. I suppose she was tucked into the flat. Perhaps a friend of hers from some society or club sat with her, I do not know. These details the therapist has left out.

There are many socially acceptable ways for a mother to grieve and I did not do a single one. I sat, dry-eyed, in a chair. If a friend held my hand or not, I cannot say. I only know that the tears, the sobs, the screaming laments of 'oh why' and 'my poor innocent baby' never arrived. The therapist has remarked on this more than once. He goes to great lengths to assert that Bart's depression is proof of 'how deeply' my husband feels, that not everyone is able to suppress her grief.'

That night, I was frozen. I did not speak. I was only partially aware of the constant movement swirling around me, the sound of hushed voices colliding into one another, my brain unable to pick them apart. I've heard people describe hurricanes, the chaos which suddenly transforms into the disturbing quiet that is like no other silence. They say this is the eye of the storm. That was my evening, of which I remember so little. Chaos, crystallised into unnatural calm.

The people left. Or hid themselves well. It must have been around 4am when Bart appeared with the sledgehammer. The image is as sharp as a photograph. I still hear the noise of his howling grief as the bathtub was shattered into fragments.

We never touched each other in those early hours before or after his rage.

I never shed a tear that night. Or at the memorial. Or the reception.

The tears come all too frequently now.

The gossips are unaware of this.

*

Solid footsteps announce Dylan's return. My fingers grip the spoon alternating between mugs, spinning the contents.

'That is quite a project, ma'am,' he says.

'Project?'

'In the washroom.'

'Yes.' There is nothing more to say. I hand him his drink, noting the remarkable cleanliness of his fingernails. Perhaps Happiness has kept that room stocked with soap. Then again, it is perfectly possibly that with so little use, the soap remains from the day Kai died.

'Thank you, ma'am,' he says.

'A pleasure.' I wrap both hands tightly around my mug. 'And it's Ella. Please.'

'Yes, ma'am, I know your name.'

My teeth imbed themselves in the ruins of my lip. We should discuss his wages. There are forms to download from the government website, to be printed out and filled in with tedious details. These will have to be faxed or scanned back. Contracts must be drawn up and photocopied. Later there will be follow-up phone calls to the agency where the advice is always to have more patience. They have no patience, however, if their payment is missed. An oversight after Kai's death. They had little sympathy.

'Is the progress of your washroom pleasing you?' Dylan asks.

There is no pleasing, unless a way could be found to remove the room from the house. The historical society would have a fit. Although none of these old homes ever boasted a bathroom in their original state. Like most, the one in the hall was once a modest-sized bedroom. Perhaps that is exactly what should be done with it. The en suite, after all, wasn't an addition, but an alteration of an old dressing room. A room for dressing, as if it were scandalous to clothe one's self in front of one's own spouse.

An image of Bart and his filthy boxers comes into sharp focus. Perhaps they did, in fact, have an excellent point.

'We are extremely water conscious,' I say, pausing to watch an ant wander across the counter. It locates the smallest of grains of sugar that missed the coffee mug. How did it know? I glance back at Dylan, who is patiently sipping his mug, as if he knows there must be more to the story. I say, 'Bathtubs use an enormous amount of water and with the system my husband has installed, it would not be able to cope.'

'Ah, so you are planning to put in a shower,' he says.

A fair comment, but surely ridiculous in the face of the obvious dust and neglect. Unless the room has been tidied, Happiness slipping in from time to time to run her mop carefully over the mess? Probably. She has her own sense of how things must be, even if pointless. The bedding in both Kai's old room and the granny flat are laundered monthly despite their lack of use.

I once tried to dissuade her.

'This is how it's done,' she said. It would have been arrogant to argue further, given that she was hired due to her expertise in domestic affairs.

'Were you looking for a new workman?' Dylan asks.

I blink. Stunned that it's this issue that has made him so bold, he who cannot tell me if he prefers his toast with butter or without. 'It is simply not of importance.'

'Ah, then I misunderstood.'

The ant is racing away with its treasure. 'How do you mean?'

'Given the state of the room, I thought work had stopped due to dismissal. The work has been poorly done.'

'I see.'

He raises his coffee to his lips, but his eyes remain focused on me. Waiting.

I owe him nothing by way of explanation. I would rather discuss why the issue matters so much to him, who probably lives without any plumbing at all. The toilet clearly still flushes; that should be enough. Yet I say, 'My husband's new water system is complicated and I am not sure –'

'My what?' Bart looms behind Dylan, curls in disarray, t-shirt creased, jeans rumpled, feet bare. But his eyes—his eyes look clear.

Dylan turns towards him. 'I was inquiring about the renovations to the washroom. I always keep an eye out for extra work. If there is no one currently on the project I wondered if I might be considered for the job.'

Bart shrugs and begins to walk towards the sink. 'Sounds fine to me. I have no interest.'

'But the water system,' I say.

Bart flips on the tap. Water gushes out. 'I'll explain it.'

I stare at all that water running directly into the drain. There is no cup or pot to catch it. 'Do you want – '

He dunks his head, catching the stream with his slightly upturned mouth. He gulps, Adam's apple bobbing, his lips making sticky noises as if consuming syrup. It goes on and on, perhaps a minute, while Dylan and I stare with mugs in our hands, until Bart abruptly straightens. Tap turned off. Droplets clinging to his curls. His mouth and cheeks moist and glistening, akin to a slobbering dog. Bart catches my stare, eyes gone wide in this most public display of slovenliness. 'What?' he says, wiping his face with the back of his hand, 'It's the only tap with filtered water.'

Of course, I think, because filtered water is of such huge importance to a man who has stopped living. The borehole water is perfectly safe; it simply tastes bad. Since when has he cared either way what something, anything, tastes like?

Bart shifts his weight and I glance down. His toenails are neatly clipped. I almost ask when he's done this, but remember Dylan still in our kitchen, still holding his mug of coffee.

'Or am I wrong?' Bart asks.

I glance up, startled. 'No, you are correct. That is the tap with the filter.'

The right side of his mouth kicks up. Not a smile, but a trace of amusement. 'Funny,' he says. He looks at Dylan. 'She can be such a wise ass. I installed the filter.'

'Of course, sir,' Dylan says.

Of course? Why of course? Has anything of my husband's demeanour indicated he does anything other than sleep?

'Anyway,' Bart says, shuffling off. 'I don't care about the bathtub, or shower, or whatever it is.' He glances over his shoulder, face now much more serious. 'If it matters to you either way, I'm fine.'

Angry laughter bursts out from my lungs. It is appalling, but it refuses to be held at bay.

He shoots me a look, then plods off.

The laughter dies.

The door slams behind him. I watch him make his way to the hammock where he flops into its gaping fabric.

'So is it settled, ma'am?' Dylan says, bringing me back to the kitchen.

'Pardon?'

'The washroom, you'd like a shower installed?'

'Oh. It appears to be so.' I glance down into my mug. The dregs spin, a gnat peppering the surface. I turn and toss the contents into the sink. They bleed into the water sitting in the basin, tendrils making their way towards the drain. Little channels, a map of some unknown land.

'Do you have an idea of what you require, ma'am?'

'Absolutely none.' The words come out firmly.

He nods, then tips back his mug, draining the contents. His Adam's apple doesn't seem to bob as pointedly as my husband's. This illustrates how truly thin Bart has become, to possess a neck scrawnier than a man who has had to beg for employment. Coffee finished, he stands. 'I'll get to work now.'

'Wait.'

'Yes, ma'am.'

'Do you actually have experience with this type of thing?'

'I've picked it up from here and there.'

'So you've never officially worked as a builder.'

'Not precisely, ma'am.' He moves to the sink and begins to rinse his own mug. Finished, he sets it on the draining board and begins to take his leave.

'Wait.'

He pauses mid-step, tilting his head back towards me.

'We haven't discussed your wages. Or gone through the forms.'

'Unnecessary,' he says, hands cutting through the air.

I stand straighter. There is no reason other than the fact that I have no words for this response. His actions are abrupt, unlike any other he has displayed today. Finite.

Then he hesitates. It is the first time I can actually imagine wheels turning in his head, rather than the dignified silence he has presented during lapses of conversation thus far. I know what it is like, to have so much to say and not want to articulate any of it. So many words swirling, their individual letters quivering, as choices must be made as to what to verbalise without saying too much. His brow furrows, perhaps selecting the words, rearranging them and setting some back before reaching for others.

He takes a deep breath, the words come softly, politely, without apology. 'Cash in hand for my daily wage is all that I require. Be best for me, and easier for you, ma'am.'

I want to argue with this statement, to explain how a proper contract is for his protection. To assure him that we'll cover the UIF tax, all two percent. But I don't, because of his accent and the colour of his skin.

I am being asked to do something illegal. A man is taking a job that could theoretically be held by another man – one legally residing in South Africa – lowering my country's spectacularly high unemployment statistics. A job that did not exist until today, until this man, this potentially illegal alien (what a dreadful term), created one. If there was no job until he existed in my home, has theft of a position actually occurred?

A tree in a forest falls and nobody hears it, comes a softly spoken reply in a crack of my conscious.

That's such a cliché, another voice says, the one responsible for the angry laughter that sent my husband off to the hammock.

But all that is said out loud is, 'You have yet to state the amount you require to be put into your hand.'

'My day's wage, ma'am,' he says.

Exasperation fills me. It must be evident because he then names an amount.

It is a fair amount. It is marginally less than what we currently pay Happiness, who has worked here for many years. Yet it is vastly higher than minimum wage.

I nod.

He dips his head in return, and then departs. The man in the hammock does not stir at the sound of the door swinging shut.

The sum returns to me. This fair amount, in a market filled with an overabundance of untrained labour. He may well be earning the highest per-day rate for a gardener in this town. Groceries tally up in my head, combi taxi fares and the cost of an occasional purchase of socks, a blanket, paper and pen. Fair amounts purchase very little. Be tricky to cover true needs, never mind wants. Still, many would envy him. Wasn't that what the xenophobia, the riots, were all about?

In the land of the blind the one eyed man is king, the little voice says.

You are full of despicable cliché, says the other.

'Yes,' I say to both of them.

*

I pad along our stinkwood floor, stopping outside the door I try so hard to studiously ignore.

A hand reaches out and touches it, running down the surface. This door is made of yellowwood, as are all of the doors in the house, along with the ceiling. None of them are exactly alike. This one has a gold streak running down the middle, while the outside is shaded with various yellows and browns. It used to make me think of a path in the old Knysna forest, light gaping between the shadows where the elephants hid. But since Kai died I can't shake the image of a tunnel. 'I saw a white light,' say the people who technically died, but didn't. That light may have called out to Kai, drawing him into its depths. Did it comfort him, or was he terrified?

My hand trembles. I clench my fist. I think of Luxolo, who always jumps into the pool, while I'm still dipping in a foot. 'Just get it over with,' he says. 'The body adjusts quicker. You're only dragging it out.'

Right.

With a gentle push the door swings open. I brace myself for the onslaught of emotion, only to be greeted with a detached sort of curiosity. It is surreal, this room, trapped in a bygone era. The bare floorboards give way to an airy space free of custom built-in cupboards. The dusty air is caught in the rays of sunlight breaking through the tall rectangular window, the antique glass slunk downward as if an ageing breast.

The reality of the space does not compare with the image I've held, that haunts my sleep. The anticipated mess of shattered fragments flung far and wide, is in actuality a forlorn dented iron tub that has lost the majority of its porcelain coating. The remains of the slick surface now lie at the base in a heap of scattered chunks, yellow and porous, the remnants of a prize-fighter's teeth. The black plastic bag, dustpan and brush that I've brought along sit heavy in my hands, useless and unnecessary.

Strangely, the destruction Bart wrought does not look out of place. Pompeii, unearthed. The bathtub could, if we so desired, be restored. What does look jarringly wrong is the blotchy showerhead, made of a cheap modern metal, which protrudes awkwardly from the wall. It was my father-in-law's one modification to the original bathroom, since his wife refused to soak in the bath.

Compassion pricks my hardened heart for a woman forced for more than twenty-five years to step in and out of the high-banked bowl despite her terrors. How cruel and needless in a room more than big enough to accommodate a freestanding shower. A sense of – remorse? – tickles the base of my skull. I never did like her. Incredibly disagreeable. The feeling was mutual, I suspect. Even so, perhaps I should have tried to understand her beyond the shadow of the man she was forced to live beneath. Maybe she was angry, resentful of her husband. I would have been. What an ego that man had. Insufferable, as the English would say. Such feelings would explain her complete disregard for the home's history when designing the en suite – tiling over stinkwood floorboards! Perhaps the en suite was her revenge.

I have always viewed her decision to bathe Kai as careless, idiotic. Why? Why! Why on earth had she done a thing when she – herself! – would never bathe? Insane. Everyone knows you don't leave a child in the bath, even to answer the phone, never mind have an entire conversation outside the room. Everyone knows. Except for her, apparently.

What kind of idiotic mother leaves her child with such an incompetent babysitter?

Me, apparently.

'She'll just play with him, read a few stories and brush his teeth,' Bart had said.

We didn't even bathe Kai every day. I'd read it dried out children's skin. That every two to three days was more than sufficient. She was aware of this, along with the fact that I had bathed him the day before. Of all the things Bart and I thought might go wrong – pjs on backwards, plonked in front of the TV, left in a dirty nappy – we'd never once thought she might attempt to give Kai a bath. It was simply unfathomable. Like snow in Mossel Bay. It simply would not happen.

Yet it did.

Bart asked her why, only once. The garbled answer revolved on wanting to be a real grandmother. As if not bathing her grandson made her less of one. She'd had no qualms shunning the deed as a mother.

They say people change. Perhaps that was it. Regret?

I certainly never regretted her death. I suspect she was grateful for it as well. Her refusal to eat was constructed as some warped penance for the part she played in Kai's death. It wasn't a suicide attempt. She stayed hydrated, and the therapist would arrange for some doctor to administer an IV. How long she would have continued in such a manner is anyone's guess. But the flu eventually gave her the out she wouldn't grant herself. I honestly thought I hated her. But now, as I reach for it, the old anger is gone. Pity. For a woman who tried to change too late and not enough.

I take a step in. Another. As I walk around the room and begin to see what this room could be. Waxed floorboards, an antique chaise lounge, a recovered copper showerhead giving way to a screed base, cubical walls decorated in mosaic tiles. The airy spaces would be filled with potted ferns sheltering birds fashioned from beaded wire. The pots would be decorated in a plain mosaic, made from the shattered porcelain that is stained yellow and slightly porous. The tiny holes bear the microscopic DNA of a person who once dwelled in me. The bathtub, however, will be banished.

The black bag, the dustpan and the brush sluice onto the floor.

I depart.

Too much. Too much. No, no, no. Too much. There are photographs to edit, there are ideas for this room to jot down, fragments of porcelain to collect, sourcing materials to research online and a man who needs to be paid. Three o'clock will be here soon enough and I still haven't packed my cossie and towel. The tasks tally up and begin to extend, spilling out of an infinite roll of parchment. Heaviness presses down, penetrating bone.

Too much.

The feet do not shuffle into the bedroom to pack a bag. The legs do not stride towards the office where the laptop, paper and pen await. Instead, the pelvis points towards the hammock whose gaping mouth cups a slumbering Bartholomew.

His bony body unconsciously makes space for another. The rocking motion, shifting with the added weight, does not set his eyelids to fluttering or cause his breath to catch. He is as accommodating as the cloth that bears the weight. With a deep breath, his scent is inhaled.

Sleep.

Eyelids dip. Visions of bruised purples and blues tinged with reds, spiked with white kaleidoscope. Rather hypnotic, begging, dragging, beckoning into the realm of rest. Each limb melts into the fabric, into Bart. Perhaps he has won. No longer matters. Another breath and the colours behind eyelids swim, rushing to the right, darting left, before curling into themselves. There is the whir of a car engine in the distance, a mournful craw from a hen, and the sound of a spade slicing into compact earth. Sounds of living, a task for somebody else.

Melting.

The breathing changes. His breath, my breath. Suddenly there are edges, I am not him, we are not us, together, dissolving. His hand, not mine, flexes on my waist, not his. I draw up a heavy hand, my hand, so we touch fingertip to fingertip, longing to melt once again.

The hammock lists, my back presses harder against his chest, the bony knob of his other wrist. I lace my fingers with his and draw his arm across me. His fingers straighten, slipping from my grasp. The arm departs, the hammock shudders with another shift of weight. The bony knob twists, palm now bearing my weight, as his body abandons mine. The hammock rights itself, his palm slips away and my eyelids open to watch his now stooped back climb up the steps to the stoep.

I shut my eyes firmly but my ears still hear the firm slap of the door against the frame.

Not even a kiss good-bye.

The tongue runs along the textured landscape of my lips. Salty. Throat contracts, swallowing saliva, setting off the internal click and boom deep within my ears. Breath becomes shallower, quieter. Skin prickles, but I refuse to move a finger in order to scratch. It is so close. Melt all on my own – right there – beyond the twisting threads of colour moving across my eyelids.

Not even a kiss good-bye.

Up, down, around, over and over again. He knew the day of the week. He clipped his nails. He set the table. So what? We've been here before.

Up, down, around over and over again. He did say I'd find another doctor. Implied that he'd go. Maybe he's merely worn out? Too much trying – too much, too much, too much. Only so much progress can be expected from one day. Too much to deal with. Too much to sort through. Too much. Too much.

Not even a kiss good-bye.

Mid-Afternoon

I hear his voice in the distance. 'Hey Dylan, good to see you here.'

'Hello Luxolo, it is good to be here.'

The hammock sways as I shift my weight in surprise. We were going to meet at the marina.

'So, they treating you alright?'

'There is plenty to keep me busy here.'

I should get up.

'Good. Good. I'm glad it's working out.'

'Yes.'

What else could he say? Perhaps much, if they shared a common language other than English.

'Hey, would you mind letting me in? I'm supposed to meet Ella.'

'I will find her for you.'

I swing my feet over the rail and shove myself upright. The earth tilts, forcing me to bend over, hands on knee. My vision narrows to a pinpoint, briefly holding steady, before widening out, bringing the grass into focus. Sucking in air, I straighten. The earth remains firm. Dashing forward, my feet skim up the steps, arm extending, ready to pull open the door.

'I'm not here.'

I swivel to see Bart slumped in a chair, feet up on the table, beer bottle dangling from fingertips. His head is pointed towards the mountains; eyes focused on something far from here.

'I beg your pardon?' I say.

'I'm not here.' He brings the bottle to his lips, taking a long pull before lowering it. Not a glance is spared in my direction.

'Who said anybody asked for you?'

'Still not here.'

I lean in, trying to catch his attention, but he remains stubbornly fixated on nothing at all.

'Listen,' he says, 'I know you and everybody are big on this intervention shit. I'm not in the mood. Just get rid of him, hey?'

'As I said before, nobody has asked for you.'

The beer bottle is raised, tilted towards the heavens. His Adam's apple bobs. With nonchalance his tongue slides out, lapping the drips from his bottom lip, leaving it moist and glossy pale, a slug's underbelly. Not a look is spared for me, his wife. Nausea lurches in my gut.

'Just making sure we're clear; I'm not here.'

Something snaps, solidifying my queasiness, sending the words sliding out, reeking of disgust: 'Never was a truer phrase spoken.'

'What the hell is that supposed to mean?'

'You said it.'

'Fucking hell. You can be such a bitch.'

Anger surges and for a dark, scary moment I visualise tossing him off the chair – sending that beer bottle flying – stomping on his head, kicking that Adam's apple into the back of his throat. The images are so vivid it is as if the deed has already been done.

'Ma'am?'

My head snaps over my shoulder. Dylan is at the bottom of the steps. Shame floods my face. His eyes find mine. 'Ma'am, Luxolo is at the gate.'

'Yes, I'll be right there,' I say.

'Still not here,' Bart says.

The door slams behind me. Adrenalin carries me across the house.

I jab the button on the intercom and shove my way out the front door. There, in the mid-afternoon November light, stands Luxolo in worn jeans and a faded black t-shirt with a slight tear to the chest pocket. Heavy black boots protect his feet. He gives me an easy grin as the gate rolls back. 'Hey,' he says, stepping across the threshold.

I send him a quick nod as my feet pepper down the steps, jaw clenched. Stopping in front of him I attempt to pull my face upwards, but only one cheek behaves, probably warping my features into a sneer.

'Good to see you,' he says.

The words do not come.

He reaches out a long toned arm anyway, drawing me closer, his lips brushing my cheek. It is a greeting extended as if all is perfectly well: as if Bart had not snubbed the meeting at noon; as if I had not stormed through the house; as if our friend were here for a braai, rather than to carry me through my first dive. I can smell the workshop in his clothes, on his skin. Metallic heat mingling with singed newspaper and steaming ink. Underneath it all is the scent of a man whose occupation demands physical labour, of sweat held at bay by the strongest deodorant. Bart used to bring home the same confectionary of aromas.

I give a solid bicep a quick squeeze and step back. 'Nice to see you, as well,' I say.

'Are you well?' He examines me up and down.

Shifting awkwardly under his scrutiny, I wonder if he can detect Bart's harsh words. Perhaps they floated to the front gate as easily as his conversation with Dylan drifted to the hammock. Or worse, perhaps my vicious craving to smash my husband's face was carved plainly on my forehead. I ask, 'And you?'

'Hanging in there.' He steps back, and motions to the grounds. 'Seems like Dylan has been busy. Lookin' good. You happy with it?'

'Yes.'

'Great. Great. I'm glad.'

I nod.

He stuffs his hands in his pockets and shrugs. 'Hey, listen. I hope you don't mind me dropping by. Just thought since the gear was already loaded and I had the time.' He shrugs. 'Maybe I could give a "hello" to Bart and –'

'Not today.'

He straightens, hands falling out of pockets. Slowly he nods. 'Okay. Sure. I wasn't going to make a big deal, it was just –'

A wave of my hand cuts him off. I study his heavy work boots. A bee is buzzing over his laces.

'Sorry,' he says.

'No, it's fine. It's only that if we're going to do this then it's better…'

'Absolutely. Not a problem.'

Glancing up from under my brow I see him nodding with far more enthusiasm than the situation deserves. 'Okay. I hope I don't seem… '

'No, no. You don't,' he says. 'I agree. Let's do one thing at a time. He blew it today. Now it is all about you.'

'Thank you.' It comes out in a whisper. Tension simmers. Underneath the anger lurked a worry that he'd push it, stride out into the back and tell Bart whatever it is Luxolo needs to say. It probably wouldn't have amounted to much at all. Bart would have stared through him, eventually stumbling into the house allowing the door to slam. Nothing more than that. At least I hope such a confrontation would never amount to more than that.

'Ella?'

'I just need to fetch my bag,' I say, turning away.

He catches my arm. 'Hey? You okay?'

I glance up. His face is filled with tender concern. With force I shove both cheeks upward, but the edges of my mouth barely follow. 'Only nerves. I'm fine. This is going to happen.'

He pulls me to his chest and now this is no longer a normal greeting. We are so close I can hear his heart beating. I can smell his scent, beyond the workshop, beyond the sweat held at bay by deodorant. I take a deep breath, savouring the essence of him. It feels good. Gratitude tugs at a marble, rocking it loose. It has been ages since somebody held me this tightly.

'You are going to be fine,' he says into my hair.

My husband said those exact words, once upon a time. He had been out with his board looking so content it was as though there was nothing else but him and the sea. Walking along the shoreline, I watched, trying to anticipate his next wave. I stumbled, plunging head first into the water. It never occurred to me he would notice. Blind fear had me thrashing, believing I was utterly alone, drowning. Yet he reached me in what must have been mere moments. Pulling me out of the water, he hauled me to his chest. He'd let me cry and splutter, never once shaming me for my panic. He didn't tease me about the makeup running down my face, or the sand smashed into my nostrils from when I had struggled to find purchase.

'You are going to be fine,' he had said into my soggy hair. His then rock-hard arms had fiercely embraced me, as if he was guarding me against my own terror. 'You are going to be fine.'

I push away from Luxolo's chest. He lets me go.

'I'm going to pop inside and fetch my bag,' I say, slipping away before he can see the melancholy that has crept in. 'Won't be a minute.'

With robotic movements, cossie and towel are located and stuffed into a canvas carrier bag. Keys and wallet follow.

Voices drift in and I remember Dylan.

'Think,' I say. 'Think.'

My mind whirls and I head towards the bathroom. Rummaging around the cupboards I locate a travelling plastic soap dish. Soap dish in tow, I march out of the house and round the corner to my office. Inside, I open the top drawer where I keep a spare clicker for the gate. In another drawer I fetch an envelope, stuffing the day's pay into its belly before sealing it shut.

Approaching the gate I see Dylan and Luxolo chatting.

A worry blooms: that Dylan overheard Bart's spiteful words. That Dylan is relaying our argument to Luxolo. My pace quickens and then slows as I remind myself that this is a man who won't divulge his real name. Who, when asking for a job, would not use his connection to Luxolo to secure the position. Dylan is discretion personified.

'Hello,' I say to them.

Dylan greets me with a nod. 'Go well,' he says to Luxolo.

'Wait,' I say, extending the envelope. 'Please, take this.'

'Thank you, ma'am.'

Heat creeps up my cheeks and I feel Luxolo's stare. 'Please, it's Ella. And here,' I hand over the clicker and the soap dish. 'All you need to do is press the button and the gate will open. Another click and it will close. Then stick it in the box and toss it over the gate.'

'Will do, ma'am.'

'It's –'

Luxolo's hand falls upon my shoulder. 'Catch you later, Dylan,' he says. Then softly in my ear, 'Leave it, Ella. He knows your name.'

I wait until Dylan is out of sight before spinning around. 'It's ridiculous, I've never been the type of person that –'

'We talking about you, or him?'

'Me.' I plunge a hand into my bag and feel around for keys.

'Then I think you've made your point clear. Nobody is judging you on this.'

'Then why does he…' the rest dies in my mouth as my fingers curl around a mass of metal and plastic. I press a button. The gate's engine whirs to life.

Luxolo nods. 'Yeah, that's about him.'

'But –'

He shakes his head as he relieves me of my bag. Slinging it over his shoulder, he begins walking towards his bakkie. 'Come on, no point in us both driving.'

For a moment I consider telling Bart I am leaving. But the fear of confrontation has me following Luxolo without good-byes. I'm being ridiculous, anyway. Bart will probably be safely back in bed before Dylan goes home. It will be fine.

I slide into the Corsa bakkie without glancing back. The interior is uncluttered. But I can detect the undercurrent of fish and takeaways. Sand lurks in the crevices, dust brushes the dash. I grasp the buckle as the seat pulls at my body, demanding wider shoulders, a flatter bum. The strap digs into my neck. I yank it forward, shifting closer to the handbrake.

The heavy door groans as it shuts. Luxolo deposits my bag at my feet. He leans forward, rolling the window down. 'Ready?' he says as the key is inserted. The engine grumbles to life. We pull off. Reaching back, he shoves the rear panes apart. Breeze plucks at my hair.

'This is a simple machine,' he says, a long finger pointing at the handle on my door, 'you got to crank it yourself.'

I allow the glass to drop.

This is a vehicle meant to be driven with its windows rolled wide open. A freedom I rarely indulge in. Too many hands slip through, seeking change, pawing for a fondle of breast. It's as if the opening is interpreted as an invitation to take liberties that have never been demanded of me when I am on foot. Yet Bart prefers me to drive.

'It's the perfect day for this,' Luxolo says over the roar of the engine and the air gushing in. 'Barely a breeze and the ocean is flat.'

We crest over the rise and begin to descend. The mountains have lost their clarity and are now cloaked in haze. But true to his word, there is no sign of the white horses that signal a choppy sea. Unusual for an afternoon, when the wind tends to pick up. We are lucky since the wee hours of the morning until noon are reserved for work. The workshop becomes too hot and stuffy to push beyond then. Although Bart, when gripped with inspiration, was known to resume work in the cool of night and press on until two, sometimes three in the morning, returning again just past five.

'Aren't you tired?' I once asked, concerned at the late hours and early dawns. This was a time before Kai, before now, a time when I knew how to sleep the night through.

'I'm in the zone,' he had said.

He attempted to explain how his work was a combination of craft and artistry. 'Look, I always know how to bang out a vase or a platter. That's routine. I know what customers want and I just do it. Probably a lot like those heart over the belly shots you hate. But to create a sculpture, I need that extra something that will allow me to speak to the glass. If I don't do it now, then I lose it. These things, that voice, it doesn't wait around.'

This elusive, intangible substance would torment him and tempt him from sleep. Inspiration. Talent. Art. The muse. It impacted his temperament. But the unpredictable moodiness was a different beast than depression. And, for whatever reason, I could accept it. At least, I could back then.

'It must be the same with the camera,' he had said.

I'd shaken my head.

'Like this shot,' he had said, pointing to a framed print of mine that had once won a rather notable prize. I had titled it *Rust*. 'This is something that requires a certain muse, that moment when you can photograph something and have it transcend what we would normally see.'

'That is how I see,' I had said.

'Yes, but your ability to see that through a camera is your art. It isn't how the world always looks.'

'Yes, it is. That's how I see. Always. Sometimes the camera can slow things down. Allow me to catch my breath. But photographs like this are always there. I simply had to learn how to make the camera capture the visions that interest me.'

'Nobody looks at the world like that.'

'I do.'

He'd gaped, then shaken his head. 'No way. You wouldn't be able to function.'

I had shrugged. 'I don't know what you want me to say.'

At the time I felt like he was telling me I was weird for having elbows or toes. How could anybody be aware that the way she views the world is artistic or not, different or not, unless outside people commented on it? I loved the camera for the way it shielded me, gave me space. The fact that others adored my work, called it art, was a mere bonus.

I shelved the camera after Kai died, ceasing my work. Exactly like Bart, I suppose. The maternity photos, the occasional wedding or christening, those were my vases. They were what brought the steady money in. It kept me feeling busy, legitimate, tempered the inheritance guilt. But after Kai died I didn't want to face strangers and their knowing faces.

Yet I'd stopped more than that, the workman-like photography. I'd ceased even the private photographs, the revelling in the art. It wasn't a conscious decision. More that my eyes slowly glazed over, dulled. All effort was put into surviving another day without Kai. Then there was my mother-in-law demanding my care as she tortured herself; Bart, wanting nothing, needing everything. Those angles, that special knack, faded. Almost as if I'd gone from being able to see with two eyes to only the one. A major shift of eyesight. I didn't notice, was too exhausted. Or perhaps I didn't care.

Until this morning. Even then, my only worries were where I'd put the camera and if it still worked. Not once since Kamala asked me to photograph her did I pause to consider that I might not be able to do anything more than take a typical amateur snap. My only reluctance was over the emotions the situation might stir up. What if that so-called-eye hadn't reopened? I simply assumed it would. Why? And I didn't even care enough to feel grateful when, with camera in hand; the world readjusted itself for me. Sounds rather egotistical. Subconsciously believing I was entitled to that artfulness when I wanted it, called upon it, *needed* it. As if my talent was nothing more than being able to ride a bike.

'I'm as bad as Bart.'

'What was that?' Luxolo leans closer.

'Nothing.'

'Sounded like you said you were as bad as Bart.'

'Nevermind.'

The bakkie swings to the left and stops. Hazards jabbed on. 'Ella? What's going on?'

'Nothing.' I motion forwards. 'Come on. I don't want to screw this up.'

'Oh no.' His hand falls on my shoulder. 'I can't have you getting upset under the water. Talk this out now.'

'No. I'm fine.'

He examines me critically. It's the same look he gives the glass, judging its worthiness for sale. 'Okay. But if it's what I think I heard, the answer is no.'

'I'm not talking about this now. I want to dive.'

'Maybe we should rethink the wetsuit.'

My gaze snaps up to meet his. 'No. I need the wetsuit.'

He holds up a hand. 'Easy now. It's only a suggestion. Hear me out. We're not going to be going deep or be in there long. The suit causes some people to freak. Makes them all claustrophobic. Given everything, maybe you should settle for a rash vest.'

'No. You said you'd arrange for a wetsuit and I want a wetsuit.'

His left eyebrow leaps up.

'Please,' I whisper.

'Hey now, it was just a suggestion.'

'Please. Go.'

*

'Hey, Erica!' Luxolo says, as we cross the tarmac to the open container that operates as the clubhouse for the local divers' club.

'Hey, you,' the woman says, squinting from her white plastic chair. 'Is that your girl?'

'Ella,' he says, turning to me, 'meet Erica. Erica, Ella. Wife of my partner and our local photographer.'

'Pleased to meet you,' she says, extending out a hand. 'Heard lots about you. But nobody mentioned how pretty you are.'

'Pleasure to meet you,' I say, taking her hand, careful not to glance Luxolo's way. Her palm is rough, the rest of her skin leathery, but her fingernails are perfectly painted in an iridescent pearl. They are so dainty and refined on a woman who has clearly never bought a tube of sun cream in her life. Early forties? Fifties? Her wild dried-out tangle of short shag surfer hair is no help: streaked in blondes

125

with touches of grey, it could easily be Bart's in a few years' time. He has never seen the point of conditioner.

'Big day for you,' she says, sizing me up and down. 'Think I've got the perfect suit.' Her voice scratches as if she smokes a pack a day. What an odd habit for someone who routinely puts her lungs under extraordinary pressure.

She stands up and begins pawing through some suits hanging on a large sturdy hook deep in the container. 'Ah, this one's good. Not too thick.' She approaches me, holding it up. 'Yeah, this is the one I think. Try it on.'

'Thank you,' I say, taking hold of the hanger.

'A pleasure.' Then her eyes dart between Luxolo and I. 'Hey, I don't want to mess in your business, but has he talked to you about wearing a suit? If this is your first time it might be best to leave it. I've got my rash with me. Happy to lend it to you.'

'No, I'm fine with the suit.'

Erica's look pins Luxolo, who tosses up his hands. 'Hey, don't look at me. She says she needs it.'

She shrugs. 'Alright, but you two do me a favour and practice in the tub a few times. Then I'm going to be nosy and watch you both from the docks. Alright?'

'Thanks, Erica,' he says. 'I really appreciate it.'

'Not a problem, hon,' she says, giving Luxolo's cheek a pat.

He smiles unselfconsciously, as if accustomed to her touch.

The changing room is an even smaller container, with a flimsy curtain dividing the space. The neoprene reaches for skin and squeezes the body in a firm hold, yet yields to movement. It does not, however, easily glide up the curves, but must be jerked into place as it sucks and grips each bit of flesh it encounters. Bart would never have looked as ungraceful as I must, stuffing my limbs in, tugging and twisting, forcing my body to accept this second skin.

'Ella, how you doing in there?' Luxolo says.

'Almost done. Zipper is sticking a bit.'

The curtain parts and he crosses over to me. He's wearing a shortie, exposing his limbs from the elbow and knee down.

Somehow this seems more personal, despite the fact that I've been in the pool with him countless times while only wearing my cossie, he in his baggies.

'Let me help,' he says, as one hand takes the zip at my lower back, the other gently brushing the hair from my neck.

The zipper slides up, pulling my body against itself. Compact. Armoured for battle.

'How does it feel?'

Safe. 'Good,' I say.

'Step out so I can check it.'

We emerge into the sunlight where I am scrutinised like a bug by Erica and Luxolo. My arms are ordered to make large circles, then swing forwards and back, while my thighs are pushed to bend deep. If I were less nervous I would crack jokes about aerobic classes. Or, if I was more me. Before Kai.

'Looks good,' Erica says, 'and I don't just mean that cute butt.'

My cheeks heat.

'Hey,' Luxolo says. 'Go easy on her.'

'I am going easy on her,' she says. 'Every woman frets about how she's going to look in a wetsuit. Why the hell do you think I got rid of the mirrors? I got sick of looking at myself. Now I just pretend I'm still in my youth.'

Luxolo laughs, 'You trying to tell me you're not twenty-nine?'

'Twenty-five, kid. Do keep up.'

I'm tying up my hair in an elastic when she stops me. 'Plait is probably best. Want help?'

'No thank you, I can manage.'

'No problem. And just remember, hey, you keep on breathing. As long as you don't hold your breath, you're good. Luxolo can take care of the rest. He's a wiz with this stuff, and that's not a compliment I give lightly.'

He shrugs off her words, but from the shift of his feet I detect that this praise has mattered.

They strap me in, tank and gadgets. She leans over to assist with the flippers, while he fusses over my mask. I thought I would feel like a seal, blubbery yet deft in the kit. Instead I think of ducks. Those creatures whose heads are rarely fully submerged, their feet rapidly churning away while their bodies glide along as if it was no trouble at all. A dip of the beak, and then they carry on. But on dry land, ducks are clumsy. Nor do they flock towards the ocean.

I take a deep breath and try to visualise the cormorant. They never hesitate to plunge deep into the sea, forty metres or more.

I still feel like a duck. Awkward and wobbly.

'Okay,' Erica says, tapping my feet. 'These are going to work. Now let's take them off. No point in wearing them in the tub.'

Thankfully the tub doesn't look anything like one. An above-ground portable pool whose water level only brushes my collarbone. We spit into our masks, dipping them in the water. Once on, the mask presses into my nose, ensuring I'll breathe only through my mouth. Mouthpiece fitted, we sink down until we are sitting on the bottom.

I blink at Luxolo, who appears as content sitting cross-legged in the base of this tub as I do sitting around a campfire. Yet, we seem apart. A barrier created by the plastic over my eyes and the jarring sound created with each inhale and exhale. Solitude, despite the crowd. It's like this each time we've sat at the bottom of a pool. Little prayers to my son form in my mind as I watch the bubbles released into the water. Some of these molecules may have touched his skin, drifted through his veins, been a part of him.

Luxolo gives me the thumbs up.

We emerge.

'Okay?' he says.

'Yes.'

He shoves the mask up to the top of his head. Peers at me. 'And the wetsuit?'

'I like it.'

'And no feeling of panic? Happy with your wet head?'

'Honestly, it is fine.' It is. Mostly.

He nods, still looking unsure.

'I'm fine. Really.'

There is something about the mask, the gear, the mouthpiece, the thick armour of neoprene, that quells the nausea that comes with having my head submerged. Without the mask it is different. Despite the practice he has put me through, despite my will that forces me under the water again and again during the lessons – teaching me to swim with my head down, taking a breath to the side – I still hate it. Regular goggles don't help. The mask does, as if one of the windows in my house separating me from the garden: the same air, but apart.

'Okay, are you ready to practice retrieving your regulator?'

I nod.

'Ella?'

No. 'Yes.'

'Okay, that's what I want to hear.'

No.

There is the moment where I have to force myself – on purpose – to release the regulator from my grip. There is the moment I catch my instinct to hold my breath. Nice and slow, I think, gently releasing the bubbles, that precious life, while reminding myself – trying to believe – that there will be more air soon. I lean slightly, extend the arm, like a ballerina, gracefully slipping through the movement, feeling the tube catch at my arms, drawing it close. Fit it to my mouth. Purge. Then it hits. The doubt. *Breathe in.* I suck as the bolt of certainty shoots through to my toes that I've screwed up, that I'm inhaling water into my lungs.

Clean, loud air expands my chest.

I'm fine.

And we do it again. And again. And again, until suddenly I shoot up.

'What's wrong?' Both his hands are gripping my upper arms tightly. His concern etched into the creases of his forehead.

I bite my lip, feeling a faint heat to my cheeks.

'Sorry. Sorry! Sorry. I just began to worry…'

'What?'

'It's…' Now I feel dumb. He would never be so careless.

'Ella? Come on now, talk to me.'

'I started to worry that I was using up all the air in the tank. That there wouldn't be enough for later, when we would be in the sea. That we were not...'

He smiles, and embraces me in an awkward, bulky, neoprene hug. 'Hey now, Erica would never let me take you into the sea without double-checking our tanks.'

He pulls back and holds up his wrist. 'Look, I've got the biggest badass watch on.' He lifts up a dial. 'I've got this gauge and look, you are wearing one too. We go in, I am holding your hand. That's my job. That's what I do with any beginner. I hold your hand. I'll be checking my watch, my gauge, your gauge. You do not have to worry. If I want us to go deeper, I'll signal you, and if you're struggling, I'll help. I want us to go up the same way. All you have to do is not panic, keep breathing no matter what, watch my hands, and let me do what I need to do.'

'Trust you.'

'That's right. You've got to trust me.'

I slowly nod.

'Is that a real yes? Or is trusting me a problem?'

Flames are eating my face, despite the cool droplets still clinging. 'It isn't that. It's...'

'It's what?'

'Letting go. To simply allow you to...Look, I have to make Bart shower. I have to actually, physically, pass over the bar of soap. I...'

He pulls me into another awkward, tight hug. I am mortified. I have never confessed this to anybody other than Kamala. Even then, I haven't divulged the details. She probably believes I simply order him to bathe. I've never explained how each step is dictated, coaxed and overseen by me. *Here is a toothbrush. Don't forget to rinse.*

'You're going to be okay.' His breath rolls over my ear. 'We don't have to do this. But I think if you do you'll feel better. It's okay to lean on friends.'

I pull back, forcing the tears to remain at bay, pulling air into my lungs. 'I'm fine.'

'Hey –'

I throw up my hand. 'No, really. I am fine. You're right, this is a matter of trust and leaning on you, and honestly, I already do it. You and Kamala and Thad and Happiness and now, probably Dylan, have all been supporting me. I do lean on people. You are all handing me soap, too.'

'Hey now, it isn't like that. And if Kamala was here, she'd say the same.'

I shrug, but know the truth. The phone calls Kamala makes; the request for photographs; the way Thad makes such a big deal over a few asparagus, a handful of strawberries and some bloated cucumbers; the way this very man, right here, has babied me as I dip my head underwater, has humoured my paranoia of a lost regulator – they are all pulling me through my days as much as I drag Bart through a shower. What Luxolo is asking, to allow him to help, has been granted over and over again despite the fact that I do not know how to let go.

'Okay, Ella. We're just going to do this a few more times and we'll be ready for the real thing. Okay?'

No. 'Yes.'

*

'You must think I'm ridiculous,' I say to Erica. She is kneeling beside me on the dock while we watch Luxolo tread water a few feet away, patiently waiting. 'I do know most people make their first dive after only an hour or so of training.'

'No honey, I don't think you are ridiculous. This is a small town. I know what happened. You have taken your time to do what you've got to do. That makes you smart. And, if I may say so, pretty damn brave.'

I kick a flipper, water sprinkles. 'You won't think I'm brave if I don't get my butt off this dock.'

'No honey, I'll still think you're brave. You're listening to yourself. You're here and you're trying. I admire that. I really do.'

I glance around. There is nobody watching. The dock is on a small inlet, tucked away from the main harbour where the big boats muscle in. The water is calm, the rock wall blocking the mild breeze. Peaceful. No holiday yachts or canoes nosing around today. Season is at least four weeks away.

'A lot of water,' I say.

'Yes, it is. But this is pretty thick stuff. Usually divers consider it a drawback, but in your case, I think you'll like it. And Luxolo, out there, isn't going to take you deep. You'll still feel the sun.'

'Okay.'

'You ready?'

I take a deep breath. Luxolo must notice, because he gives me a thumbs up. I nod. 'Ready.'

'Alright. Now, just remember what I told ya, turn around and just drop in. Then onto your back and let him tow you out a bit.'

I wince. 'I can swim.'

'And I believe you, or I wouldn't be letting you go out there. But that's how we do it here. No fancy back flips off a boat for a newbie – that's for any newbie who comes through my club – not just you. We like to make sure you are at a good spot before we take you down. Okay?'

'Okay.'

She pats me on the shoulder. 'Good girl.'

'And you want my regulator in now.'

'Yes, honey, I really, really do. Don't worry; I checked your air. You're not gonna run out. And frankly, even if the whole damn thing came off, you could just dog paddle back here. Got it?'

I nod, feeling lame. Ridiculous. It really is right on the shore, stone pebbles lining the bank, easy to scramble up if I so desired. I am hemmed in. Except not. A glance to my left and I see water stretching all the way to the mountains that guard the other end. The Great White breeds here. Whales come with their young, breaching towards the clouds. Dolphins and seals routinely surf the waves amongst the people. This little spot by the dock may be no more than a pond, but if I drifted out through the gap I'd be in the wide open deep.

'Don't look that way, honey. Focus on the man waiting for you.'

The mouthpiece is fitted. Deep breath and I turn to the side; place both palms down on the dock.

One. . .

Two. . .

Three. . .   I flop in, heavy, graceless, water splashing across my mask and onto Erica's feet. But she is standing there clapping anyway as I bob like a floundering sack, heart hammering away.

A hand comes down on my shoulder.

'Tip back!' Erica yells, but the words are dulled by the respirator, even above water.

I tilt, the heavy tank happy to pull me the rest of the way. There is a tug, then my bulk glides. Slows. Another tug. Glides. Slows. Above me is the clear November sky, watching. I'm doing it, I silently whisper to that faceless blue observer.

We stop. I feel myself being released. A swirl around me. He is there, in front. He reaches out and takes something from my vest. Then he presses it into my hand.

We've done this. I press when he tells me and we'll sink. I've assured him I am happy to do this part.

He gives me thumbs down.

I give the okay.

He takes up his own in his hand.

One…

Two…

Three…   We sink. For a moment I am alone. The loud noise thrumming in my ears, the light pushing through the cloudy murk that has closed over my head, saturated my hair.

Breathe, Ella. Keep breathing.

His hand finds mine and grips it tight. He won't let me go. Strong, sure, a hand that rotates heavy rods, rolling glass back and forth at even speeds, without letting it drop. He won't let me go, he won't let me go.

A kick of a fin and we become one, sliding along the water's thick crust, a shimmering layer of stew where the sun still filters in, bent by the water's command. We drift along, occasionally dipping deeper. He reaches out to show me what I may touch. A fist to alert if something is dangerous. Guiding my hand toward a creature of interest. I should be eager to explore, but there is no energy to care. It's like looking through a dirty tank, colours muted and bland.

This should be a momentous occasion. I, Ella, who made it a personal policy to never dunk my head underwater, am scuba diving. I have triumphed over my fear, my terror, my nausea, and am calmly floating in the sea. Even Old Ella couldn't do this.

I should be pleased. Victorious.

I have never felt so alone.

There is only Luxolo's hand gripping mine, the sound of the regulator, the armoured safety of the neoprene and the murky cloak of the water.

Nothing else.

I thought he would be here: beside me, under me, around me as I allowed the sea to wrap each leg, arm, the belly, the head. I thought that through the loud din of the regulator would be the whisper of his laugh. I imagined he would solidify into the perfect image of his face – so clear I'd reach out and stroke a liquid cheek, tousle a watery curl, kiss his lips. For a moment he'd be whole. We would touch. All would be possible, if only I submerged myself in this wet, salty mass of murky secrets.

I know he dwells in the soil, infiltrating strawberries, working his way into the asparagus. I feel him in the chard. Spoonful by careful spoonful, I've fed his ashes into the earth, to *become* once again. With each bite, he moves on, into me, Bart, Happiness, into customers who step through Plato's Bru.

I can smell a hint of his chubby feet, the fresh scent of his hair each morning when I etch my love into the sand. As the water devours the words, pulling at my ankles, drawing me closer, I assumed he was here, more than anywhere else. Waiting. Patiently. For his mother to brave the deep beyond. Completely.

Here, in this bay, there is only the brush against the cheek. A slip between my fingers. A caress along my wrist. Just as it is when I do the dishes or water a plant. The whisper along my forehead is no louder than when I shower under the tiled marble glare of energy-saving bulbs. The scent is no stronger in the ocean than it is in my everyday. This murk is full of cloudy organisms, fish excrement, plant matter and ship debris. There is even an oily trail of memories. But my son is not here as I had hoped.

*

I flop onto the dock, a gasping fish that has never before touched land.

'Easy honey, I've got you,' Erica says, as her strong hands with iridescent nails grip my vest and haul me upright.

She takes the regulator and eases it away from my spluttering mouth, then tips me upright. Beside me, Luxolo presses his palms against the dock. He springs up, turning his body in the air, and softly comes down next to me. Practiced gracefulness that looks so easy, natural. He looks relaxed, content. He gives me a wink, as he lays a hand on my thigh.

'Well done, Ella! Well done.'

I cannot speak.

Erica peers at me. 'Lips are a bit blue. We'll get you into the showers and then a nice hot cup of tea. You'll soon feel more like yourself.'

I give a slight nod, then my body shudders.

'No panic?' She eyes Luxolo.

'She seemed fine. Calm. No problems.' He squeezes my thigh. 'Ella?'

I nod. The trembling won't stop.

Erica brushes a strand of hair from my forehead. 'She's going to be just fine. Right, let's get her to that shower, and after that, I suggest you stuff some food into her.' She taps my knee. 'Here we go hon, give me a foot.'

They dote on me as if I am a small child, tenderly relieving me of my flippers. Erica slings my vest over her shoulders, ignoring the wet, and begins to walk up the ramp with my flippers dangling from the tips of shimmering fingers.

Luxolo takes my hands and helps me to my feet.

'Ella?'

I turn my head towards the mountains. My teeth have begun to chatter, knees threatening to fail. I may throw up. But I cannot find it in me to care.

'Ella,' he says. 'Oh, Ella. I'm sorry.'

Tears begin to fall. Gobs of them, rushing down my salty face.

He pulls me into his chest. His arms wrapping around me, holding me up. His hand cradles my head, stroking the sodden hair, as he gently rocks me. 'Shh, it's okay. It's okay. All going to be okay. . .'

Back and forth he sways, holding me up, tight against his chest. The tears keep pouring. So many shed today: in frustration, exasperation, desperation. But the ones flooding out now come from a place far deeper. A spot where I had stashed that hope I had never confronted or acknowledged until I allowed the sea to swallow me.

'Shh…'

I'll *never* have him back. Never, ever again. Always thought Poe was being overdramatic when his blasted raven crowed, 'Nevermore.' So smug was I, back in my teens, mimicking

'Nevermore, nevermore, oh boo hoo. Get over it.' Then my friends and I, to our poor English teacher's disgust, would snicker.

Nevermore.

What I've had since he died is all that I will ever have. As time goes forward, there may be even less. All that I can do is continue to bless him with a world tour, a bit in a cucumber, another molecule lingering in some stranger's freshly squeezed lemonade.

Nevermore.

'Shh…'

Nevermore.

'Shh. Ella. I'm right here. Going to be okay.'

A shaky breath steadies my lungs. My eyes begin to blink back the water, dampening the flow.

'I'm sorry,' I choke out.

'Were you scared?' His words are so soft, but his grip has not lessened.

I twist my head back and forth along his chest. 'No. No. I wasn't scared.'

'Okay.'

His hand continues to stroke my head. Our bodies sway with his rhythm.

'You going to tell me what's wrong?'

Another shaky breath pulls the water back. My eyes seal shut. Luxolo stops moving. So still. Quiet. Until my ears detect his heartbeat. And yet he waits.

'It…'

His arms tighten.

'I …' Even now, I can't say the raven's words out loud. 'I was lonely.'

He doesn't say a word, but his hand on my head presses firmer. Perhaps what I've said is enough. It is enough. You don't need much to keep on living. Look at Bart.

A kiss on my head. 'Let's get you into the shower,' he says.

Quietly, we walk up the dock's ramp. He doesn't let go of my hand until we reach the outdoor showerhead, tucked behind the changing container. With a squeeze, he lets me go. He turns me and lowers the zip to the wetsuit, air brushing my exposed skin. With that, he wordlessly walks away.

Alone, I claw out of the neoprene, ripping my limbs from its grip. It plops into a pile on the gravel. I give the wetsuit a kick. It flops over without protest. I want to lash out at something. Anything. But nothing presents itself.

Shivering in my cossie, I turn the tap on. The small showerhead produces a surprisingly hot stream. It is fresh, clear and clean. Relief spreads as the water sluices over me. It eases the tension in my neck, shoulders and lower back. Salt is rinsed from my hair, and rubbed off my skin. Fingers, toes and lips tingle back to life. My heartbeat returns to its typical pace and the wrenching ache begins to dull. It never completely dissipates. But this is more like what I carry in the everyday. This I can bear.

The crunch of the gravel alerts me to Luxolo's presence. 'Brought your towel,' he says, as he places it on a hook just out of the shower's spray.

'Thank you.'

'A pleasure,' he says, leaning over and picking up the wetsuit. 'I'm just going to rinse this and give it back to Erica. Okay?'

'Thank you.'

He straightens. Eyes bore into me. I expect him to say something. At least something more than what he eventually does say, 'Erica's got the tea ready.'

'Thank you.'

He departs with the wetsuit. The water continues to pelt my skin. At home my showers last around four minutes for a basic scrub, eight if washing my hair. I rarely ever indulge for as long as ten. Each minute, on average, sends 19 litres of water chugging down the drain. Which is why there is always a feeling of guilt when I shower twice after using the pubic pool, even though the first shower is merely a two minute rinse and I keep the double wash of my hair to the allotted eight. Yet today I cannot force myself to step out of the stream. I have no soap, razor or shampoo. There are only my hands stroking my limbs under the light, clean spray. A need to shed the despair that lurked in the bay.

Minutes tick by.

Fifteen.

Sixteen.

Nobody comes by to order me out. But at eighteen my hand shoots out, cutting it off. An instinctive limit that says I've indulged too much. The craving for more causes the skin to bristle, my cheeks to scrunch up. The light breeze plucks along each follicle, raising goose bumps. Wrapping my towel tightly, I scamper into the dressing container.

The clothes tangle themselves between my limbs. I have to concede defeat and sit on the ground before shoving each leg into my jeans. To secure my bra I must hook from the front and slide it around before pulling the straps into place as I did when I was thirteen. For a moment I am lost in my vest. It takes four tries to work the zip on the jacket.

When I finally emerge Erica is alone, sitting in the white plastic chair. 'Hey honey, I've boiled the kettle for you.'

She pushes to her feet, and motions to the chair. 'Sit yourself down. I'll fetch our mugs.'

'Oh, I'm fine. I don't need to sit.'

She casts a pointed look over her shoulder. 'Honey, I've got more chairs. Sit.'

I sit.

The air has grown still. Quiet has cloaked the late afternoon air. The clouds that have skirted past Mossel Bay have collected themselves around the mountains. Tonight will probably bring a spectacular sunset. The kind that once would have led to Bart and I sitting side by side on the stoep, my head resting against his shoulder, tucked under his chin, as our gazes focus west.

'Here ya go, hon,' Erica says, pushing a warm mug into my hands, her other arm pressing an identical chair to her hip.

I accept the mug. The plastic chair thuds beside me.

'Think I'm going to fetch myself a beer,' she says, striding away.

I hold up the large white mug. Written in black bold font, it says: 'Divers Enjoy Going Down.'

Bart used to adore blowjobs. He never treated them as an expectation or took them for granted. His gratefulness, his appreciation, had always been so charming. He made me feel sexy. I felt powerful and they were rather fun. I cannot even begin to imagine what Bart would do if I tried to pull such a stunt now. Would he merely lie there until I grew weary of it flopping around in my mouth? Or would he shove me away, darting across the bed faster than I've seen him move in months?

'Like my mug?' asks Erica from deep in the container.

'Of course.' But the tea is dreadful. The bag was probably left to steep during my entire shower. Even the heavy spoons of sugar cannot mask the thick cloying tannin.

Sugar.

My whole body shudders. This is funeral tea.

'Drink up, honey,' Erica says, sliding into the empty chair.

The look she gives me says she will not tolerate argument. Despite the taste, despite the horrid associations, I take a gulp, trying to keep my face from showing my disgust. I blame my boarding school upbringing for my submission.

'That's it. Good girl. Get the whole mug in.'

My tongue shrivels at the thought. Yet each choked gulp sends a soothing warmth radiating from belly to limbs. Sugar and caffeine work their way into my veins and by the time the entire concoction is consumed my shaky disposition is settled. The hollows less vulnerable, my nerves less exposed.

Erica gives a nod of approval. 'Nasty stuff, but it can calm anything. Me, I'm more of a coffee drinker. But for some things, you can't beat a strong cup of sweet tea.' She takes a swig from her bottle.

Decorum is overrated. 'It's revolting.'

Hearty laughter erupts out of her smoky lungs. 'Absolute kak, honey. But if you're feeling more like yourself, I'm happy to bring you a beer.'

'Thank you, but I'm fine for the moment.'

'Probably wise. Trying to remain calm and not panic uses up a ton of energy and can really do a number on the nerves.'

'I didn't panic,' I say. 'Honestly, I wasn't scared.'

'I believe you,' she says.

'It was only that, emotionally, I wasn't expecting what … what it was.'

She takes a big pull from her beer before setting the bottle down next to her chair. 'Honey, my ex-husband – a real asshole, bless him – is a big mountain climber. All these rock-jocks climbing way up high in order to find something, beat something, or run away. Hell, my ex is still trying to prove something to God-only-knows. And I've heard others claim being up there brought them closer to Jesus. The universe. Whatever. But I'll tell you, hon, there is nothing like scuba diving to make you face yourself. It's just you in that vast openness, moving on borrowed time thanks to that tank of air. I imagine the only thing that comes close to matching it is being in outer space.'

Or giving birth, I think.

She picks up the bottle, and drains it. 'Sure you don't want one?'

I shake my head.

She walks off with the empty.

Two pigeons land close to my left with red-rimmed eyes. They begin to frantically peck the gravel. Every year there seems to be more of them. It wouldn't surprise me if their numbers have surpassed the gulls. I've tried to understand why so many locals love to keep these birds. But they seem as useless as my mother-in-law's ponies.

Erica returns, sliding next to me. 'My, my, this is going to be a beautiful evening. Probably the best we've had this spring.'

I give a polite nod as I inwardly cringe. I've managed to sink so low that even Erica is talking about the weather. But she is right; the air does hold that promise of braai season. Bart used to love to cook over a fire. He went beyond tossing boerewors, sosaties and the occasional steak over the flames. He would stuff aubergines, grill marrows and wrap fish into palm leaves. The fish always came out perfect: juicy and full of flavour. This in stark contrast to my attempts, which often end up drier than today's scrambled eggs.

A crunch of gravel announces Luxolo's return. He crosses onto the tarmac, the sunlight catching the stray droplets that have clung to his tight, closely-cropped curls. He looks fit, healthy, confident. Strong. As if the events of the day have not weighed him down. Mine do. Every day. All those marbles.

'Hey, hon,' Erica says, 'Can I get you a cup of tea? Beer?'

'I'm alright, thanks,' he says, coming to a stop by my chair. 'You ready to grab something to eat?'

It takes a moment before I realise he is speaking to me. 'I hadn't thought about it.'

'Really? Because I'm starving. Diving always does that to me.'

My stomach grumbles.

'Heard that,' he says.

'Me too,' Erica says, as she presses the bottle to her lips.

'Come,' he says, giving my chair a soft kick, 'I'm treating you to a fine meal at the Sea Shack.'

Erica laughs. 'Ja, hon, you sure know how to treat a lady right.'

'Hey, I need the grease.'

'Some people get all the luck,' she says. 'I even look at that stuff and I gain a kilo. But hey, enjoy! They've got a special on today: buy one basket, second half price. Can't beat that.'

'Great,' he says. 'Now I look cheap.'

'Hey hon, you know what they say, if the shoe fits.'

Luxolo holds out a hand, which sends Erica into peels of smoky laughter.

He turns to me, 'Come on Ella, let's go.'

I push out of the chair and blink wordlessly at Erica. I should say something. Thank you would be a good start. But I say 'thank you' when a cashier gives me my change or when the post office hands over a parcel.

'Give me a hug, honey,' she says, and pulls me into a bosomy, cigarette-scented embrace.

'Thank you,' I say.

'Really good to meet you,' she says, with an extra squeeze.

'A pleasure to meet you, as well,' I say, pulling away.

'And take care of yourself.'

'Um, you too.'

Luxolo begins to tug me away. I scramble after.

'And give Bart my love,' she shouts.

I trip on a thick slice of air. Luxolo catches my arm. 'Easy now,' he says softly. Then he lifts up his other arm and gives a big backwards wave. 'You'll feel better after some food.'

'I had no idea she knew him,' I say, as my legs recall how to walk.

'Small town.'

I nod. But it isn't that simple. Another reminder that Bart once had a life full of friends and acquaintances: people who hung out around the workshop, people who loved the sea as passionately as he. These were people who I rarely saw or didn't know existed, while I rushed around promoting my trade at nurseries, crèches and baby boutiques. A world that was outside my sphere of meeting gallery owners, entering contests and debating lighting, filters, angles and composition on a handful of chat boards. Now his world has shrunk to only me, and it is glaringly apparent I am not enough.

EVENTIDE

'You want to talk about it?' Luxolo says, tilting his beer glass and giving the contents a swirl.

I shake my head.

A gull with one leg hops towards our picnic table under the tatty blue awning next to the seawall. It seems impressive – springing around on one foot across a balance beam stretched along the pounding waves – until one remembers that it has the option of flight. It parks itself less than an arm's length from my face and tilts its head, beak opening and shutting in case we've missed its point. Our food has yet to arrive. This appears to have no impact on its expectations. So much hope. Or optimism. Does it miss its leg? Or is it merely pleased to still be alive? Perhaps it has forgotten that it once had two. Maybe, for this bird, one leg is simply the way things are.

'I swear this is the same seagull that was at my table last time,' Luxolo says, raising his glass.

'Gull.'

'What?'

'You are supposed to refer to them as gulls, since some breeds are found away from the sea.'

The glass pauses as he shakes his head. 'No, this bird is a seagull, it is right here next to the sea. Any damn closer and it would be wet. Those other birds are simply confused. Hey, happens to the best of us.'

'Denying it doesn't make the fact less true.'

'Names are arbitrary and can be changed. What's that famous dead guy say? A rose by any other name still stinks.'

I raise my brow.

'Or something like that,' he says, waving me off. 'My point is, that this bird lives by the sea. Seagull.'

'It also seems to live by a table, like a pigeon. Nothing but a table pest.'

'Table pests. I like it. Maybe I'll start using that as my new word for pigeons. Those damn things shit over everything. Drives me crazy.'

I smile into my wine.

'I see that,' he says.

I sip my drink, refusing to comment.

The waiter arrives with two baskets brimming with chips, deep-fried battered mushrooms and what the Sea Shack swears is fish. I'm dubious, but Luxolo has assured me that anything can be cured with enough salt, vinegar and tartar sauce.

The waiter claps his hands together loud enough to startle our one-legged gull. 'Can I get you anything else?'

I open my mouth to order a takeaway for Bart and then pause. By the time I get home the sun may be setting and he will be tucked away for the night. Then my fridge will be full of leftover fish. The mere thought is dreadful enough.

Luxolo taps my hand, 'Ella?'

'No, I'm fine, thank you.'

The waiter walks away.

Perhaps I should phone Kamala and have her check to see if he is okay. She could fix him a marmite sandwich if he needs. Or not. She'd probably call me an enabler. He'll be fine. Perfectly capable of feeding himself if he tried.

The gull resumes its place. Luxolo tosses it a chip. It springs up; catching it mid-air then lands to give me a pointed look.

I stab a mushroom-like blob and bring it up for inspection.

'No, no,' he says, 'this kind of food is supposed to be shovelled in.'

'I'm not sure –'

He inserts a forkful of something into my mouth: a crunchy vinegary tang laden with salt takes over my tongue. It slips down my throat and hits my stomach with a thud.

'Ah, now you're a real scuba diver,' he says.

A grin escapes.

'So it wasn't a total bust, then?'

'The actual diving part was fine, actually.'

'Ja, okay.' He pops a clutch of chips into his mouth.

I poke at mine with a fork. I do not understand the local adoration for limp and soggy chips. They have so little dignity, or potato. I like them thick and strong, standing tall, practically on the verge of being a wedge. This would be the perfect subject to distract Luxolo. But as the words are ready to escape, it occurs to me that the last time I heard the phrase, 'thick and strong, standing tall' it was being said by a very drunk Kamala. She hadn't been referring to potatoes.

A gentle heat that belies the cooling air pools in my cheeks.

'Wine getting to you?'

'Been a long day.'

'Kamala mentioned you took some snaps this morning.'

An image of my friend standing unabashedly naked comes into focus, deepening the heat in my cheeks.

'Hey, no need to be embarrassed. I'm glad you're getting back into it. You've got a real knack. Plenty of your work still up in the workshop.'

'I haven't been there in ages.' My voice is thick with apology.

'It's not your problem. Kamala is right. The guys and I are going to make a plan. You just keep doing what you're doing. It's working.'

No, it isn't.

The gull caws. I toss it a chip. It hops down on the bench next to me. I give it another.

'You can't come home with me,' I say. 'The chickens would never forgive me.' I place a handful of the greasy worms beside me. The gull fluffs its feathers in obvious delight.

'Now that's what I really miss,' he says. 'The fresh eggs being brought to work.'

'I'll give you some when you drop me off.'

'That would be good.'

'It's the least I could do, after everything you've done.'

'Hey,' he says. Voice gone soft. Serious. 'I wanted to. Honoured. You really impressed me today.'

A crack about soaking his neck with all my excessive sobbing would be appropriate here, but my entire vocabulary becomes jammed between the marbles wedged in my gut. So I pick up my wine and drink, despite being well aware that my attempt at nonchalance is fooling no one.

But yes, underneath my disappointment, the aching hole, there does lurk an underlying pleasure to have followed through with the dive. The actual enjoyment of the act was lacking. I suppose it is much like when Dorothy Parker said, 'I hate writing, I love having written.' I am pleased with having scuba dived.

'I'm never doing it again,' I say.

Luxolo eyes me over his beer.

'I know I told Erica I might, but I will not.'

'Hey, it's not a problem. It isn't for everyone. Just the fact that you tried it is amazing.'

I fiddle with the stem of my wine glass. 'I hope you don't feel…' The gull hops forward as if hanging on my words. A few chips still remain on the bench.

'What?'

I turn my attention back to him. 'After all that time you spent with me in the pool, it must seem a bit of a waste. I am sorry about that.'

'Hell no, it's not a waste. Don't say that. I enjoyed it. I enjoy spending time with you.'

My skin prickles under the words. I hastily reach for my wine.

The gull glares. I pass it my basket.

'You're going to kill that damn thing,' he says.

'Entirely possible.'

He motions to the waiter for the bill.

I look across the bay. A lone kayaker soundlessly glides along the water. Rather brave, given the Great Whites are supposed to be most active during the changes of the day: sunrise, sunset. A crew once caught the sharks breaching on film for some international documentary. The whole town talked of nothing else for weeks. Perhaps the kayaker believes that it will never happen to him. That shark attacks only happen to those other people. Bart never worried.

'You can feel it when it's sharky and then you just don't go in,' he once said.

'That doesn't make sense,' I said.

'That's because you never go in the sea.'

I did today. Admittedly, once I was actually in the water I never gave a passing thought to the sharks. Perhaps it was because we were so close to the dock. Or they simply were not around.

Or because facing the emptiness was far worse.

The waiter arrives with the bill. I take it, only to have Luxolo snatch it.

'This should be my treat,' I say.

'Don't hurt my man pride,' he says, stuffing some bills into the black folder before returning it to the waiter. 'Cheers,' he says and the waiter departs.

I turn back to the bay. I feel his gaze following mine. 'Sun's going to set soon,' he says. 'Hey, why don't we watch it from my place?'

I should check on Bart. 'Sounds fine,' I say.

*

We climb the stairs of the soulless block of 1970-esque flats slammed between the original sandstones. Given the passion of the historical society, it is a wonder that these things were ever granted planning permission. Yet here they are, overshadowing the beauty of the older structures, admittedly with a very nice view of the bay. And other people's laundry. And the impoverished souls, wedging themselves into defunct bus shelters and grotty overhangs. Makes this place one of the more reasonable rentals, if one desires a view.

Outside Luxolo's door the air is thick with urine, beer and the sickly sweet odour of dagga. Inside is the same stark, sterile environment I recall from my last visit. A table with one chair. A brown two-seater sofa in front of the TV and stereo system that are sitting on crates. There is the hook for his wetsuit and shortie. There is space for the boogie board, the diving equipment behind the sofa. Unless things have changed, his bedroom holds a basic double bed, a pine set of drawers, a narrow matching wardrobe. There are no pictures or posters on the walls. There is no sign of his work on any surface.

I once asked why his flat was so bare.

'It's a rental,' he had said, as if such an answer was enough.

'But not even a homey touch here or there? A piece you made at work?'

'Why? If it is that good, then it should be for sale. I'm saving up.'

I never asked what he was saving for. It seemed rude. Nosey. Still does, actually.

He tosses his keys onto the table. 'Take a seat outside. I'll just get the drinks. Wine?'

I nod.

The modest balcony is a bare cement slab with basic iron bars. A stack of white plastic chairs, identical to those at the diving club, are shoved in a corner. It is difficult to pry them apart. My fingers dig deeper until, with a final shake, the top chair gives way with a slight gasp as the air rushes to fill the empty space.

I sit down. The sky to my left is beginning to brighten with electric pinks and blues. Orange shoots under the belly of some of the clouds, whose scattered, broken patterns remind me of lily pads taking over an English pond.

A glass is proffered over my shoulder. 'I only have red.'

'Thank you.' I take the glass. It is chilled to the touch. 'Do you keep it in the fridge?'

'Oh, don't you start. It's the way I like it, hey?'

Which is an excellent point. Why should a person do or drink something simply because that is the way somebody somewhere declared it to be so? It's his wine; he enjoys it this way. In fact, the next time I eat sushi I will not apologise for eating it with a fork. Which will still be awkward, given that I typically eat sushi with Kamala and she is perfectly at ease with chopsticks.

Bart won't eat sushi. 'And don't give me shit about it,' he said the last time he turned down my invitation to join in. 'You, who won't eat leftover cooked fish, cannot look down on me for not wanting to eat the stuff raw.'

In retrospect that was a rather normal, almost chipper, conversation. Normal aside from the fact that one of us was tucked in bed at five in the afternoon. Blinds drawn. Still trying to 'muster the energy' to shower for the day and had only eaten a slice of toast that I'd fetched for him, unasked.

A white plastic chair settles next to me. Luxolo folds himself into it, with ease. 'Perfect evening,' he says.

I nod, holding my chilled red wine to my chapped lips. They'll probably be stained purple. The dry skin absorbing the tannin.

'Such colours,' he says. 'Every time there is a sunset like this I try to memorise it. But when I get to the workshop it never turns out right.'

'Why not?'

He leans forward, as if he might reach out and brush his fingertips along the sky's paint. 'I think it's because the glass is too solid,' he says. 'Or thick. Not sure. And, of course, I don't have constant control of how light hits it.'

'Even on lampshades?'

'Those can actually look the worst.'

'Why? I like them.'

'It is like trying to light up the sky with a streetlamp or a spot light. Totally different effect. Which is why I always make them in colours that have no resemblance to sunsets.'

I'd never considered that. Could perhaps explain why Bart always sneers at stained glass pieces that depict scenes with mountains and the rising moon.

The sky shifts and the colours begin to dull. Smokey shadows encroach upon the clouds. This is often when I'll spot an owl. I sit on our stoep almost every evening. Being in the house this time of day is too hard. My body gets restless. As if the molecules and traces of old hormones are still programmed to read bedtime stories, brush tiny teeth, plant a kiss on a wee forehead. On the stoep I can shut up the voice with a glass of wine. Or two. Perhaps more if the day has been particularly harsh.

Bart never joins me. Not once.

'You've hardly touched your wine,' Luxolo says.

I glance down into my glass. The red is growing dark. I think of vampires and old medieval goblets with hammered angles, heavily jewelled. There was a period in school where I read nothing but fantasy and sci-fi. Now I hardly pick up a book. I can no longer handle the unexpected emotions. Even the fantasy world is wracked with tragedy. Too close.

'Okay,' he says. 'Next time I'll try to remember to keep a bottle out of the fridge.'

'It's fine,' I say, and take a sip. It slides down easily enough.

'You do not have to drink it to humour me.'

'No, really, this is fine.' The sky is darkening. I shiver. 'Think I'm cold.'

'Then let's take our drinks inside. Show's over, anyway.'

I nod.

We settle on the sofa. There is nowhere else to sit aside from the solitary folding chair at the small table.

'Warmer?' he asks.

I nod, my body hunched over itself. It is only November. By February the evenings will be a relief from the blistering day. But for now, the downside to a comfortable spring day is the nip of the night.

'I've got a floor heater,' he says.

'No really, I'm fine.'

He stands up and swiftly exits the room. I hold the glass to my lips, little tastes on the tongue. It has nothing to do with the cooling of the air or the oddity of drinking chilled red. There simply isn't the yearning for alcohol, which permeates the majority of my evenings.

A heavy weight descends on my shoulders, full of the scent of man. 'This should keep you warm,' he says, patting the dark green fleece of the blanket so that it tucks down between the sofa and my back.

He settles next to me, slipping an end around his own body. He smiles. 'This is better.' I follow the column of his throat as he swallows.

The movement is fluid, cresting over the Adam's apple, rather than jerking it up and down in a disgusting bob.

His eye catches mine. 'Hey,' he says, soft. Warm.

'Hey.'

His finger traces lightly on my jaw. 'Still not drinking.'

'Don't need to,' I say.

'What do you mean?'

'I'm simply enjoying this.'

'What's this?'

'Not being alone at night. Companionship. It's rather nice.'

His finger presses firmer. My lips part slightly. I say, 'What do you normally do in the evenings?'

'Oh, you know.'

No, I don't. It's been too long since I ventured out past dinnertime. There is always the need to check on Bart. To see if his chest still moves in its rhythmic rise and fall. Then I take myself out to the stoep and listen to the frogs click while the bats swoop and arch, chasing their prey.

His finger is still tracing my jaw, running along the edge of the bone. His body heat is beginning to press against mine.

A realisation dawns that he would like to kiss me but will not. This is as far as he will go. This is simply something I know, perhaps in the same way that Bart knows the shark will not bite. We will sit here, Luxolo and I. He, touching my face with one long finger. A finger that grasped my hand tightly as we pushed ourselves under the ocean's skin. This is all he will ask of me.

I miss kissing. Not the brief press of lips to the crown or forehead, a brush against the cheek. But those kisses when lips touch, warm, companioned, tasting one another, creating heat.

So I lean over and do it. My lips against his, which are so much softer, healthier, than my own. He doesn't pull away. Other fingertips slide up my jaw, along my cheeks, until they've slipped into my hair, holding me against his pliant warmth. The marbles in my gut melt. My tongue reaches out and meets his.

A soft moan of relief escapes. I've needed this, affection, for so long. He is so perfect. Yet as his other arm circles my body and presses me closer to him, I know I can't follow through.

I continue kissing him anyway. Parts of me that have felt deadened stir, tingling, ready to be used, touched, penetrated. He would allow me to spend the night. Bart would probably never guess. It feels so good. I've missed this more than I've ever admitted until this moment. Lips on mine.

My hands cup his face, his beautiful trusting face, and hold him a few more moments. Memorising this feeling of being desired.

I pull away.

My heart leaps out, trying to snatch him back.

'I'm sorry,' I say, almost choking on the words. 'So, so sorry.'

'Hey,' he says, his thumb brushing my cheekbone. I want to nuzzle in, follow the curve of his palm.

'No.' I carefully take his hand and remove it. My skin weeps and begs me to change my mind. 'I shouldn't have done that.' It comes out in a whisper.

'It's okay,' he says.

I shake my head. 'No, it isn't and it's my fault.'

'Hey, I'm not going to pretend my inviting you back here was entirely innocent. This isn't all you. I would enjoy it if you stayed with me tonight.'

Yes. 'I can't.'

'You could, but you won't.'

'Precisely.'

He looks crushed. 'Because you're married. Is that it? Because from what I can see, it isn't much of a marriage.'

True. 'Far more complicated than that. So much so.'

'What?'

I shift back, as much as the sofa will allow. He lets me. 'I'm sorry. I led you on and –'

'No, it isn't like that. When I'm around you there is something different. I enjoy your company.'

'Pickings are slim around here, I understand.'

'Hey, don't sell yourself short like that. You are an incredible person and it hurts like hell to see you miserable and being treated the way he's – no, I shouldn't go there. But Ella, I care. I truly care about you.'

My eyes squeeze shut while my chest tightens. This isn't fair. I haven't been fair. I'm not the person he imagines me to be. 'I cannot have this conversation right now. Sorry. Again, I know I started it. But I can't.'

'Hey, I get it. Don't worry.'

I shake my head. He doesn't get it. Because right now, even if Bart and I were no longer us, it would change nothing. I'm too much of a mess. I should watch some of those videos Bart bought or look up porn on the internet. Not manipulate a trusted friend to fill a hole that has no end.

'Please, Ella. Don't be upset. We're good.'

'I've ruined our friendship.' As soon as the words are out, I know this is true. We will no longer meet up for a cup of coffee. Take a walk on the beach.

His hand slides up my arm and gives a gentle squeeze. 'Ella, look at me. You haven't ruined anything. We simply poked at a boundary, that's all. Just establishing where it is for now.'

It's the 'for now' that stings the most.

I've been selfish.

I gave him hope.

NIGHTTIDE

There is only the rumble of the bakkie as he drives me home. As I pop open the door he reaches over, capturing my wrist. He doesn't say a word, allowing the gentle squeeze to say enough. I bow my head, a player on stage who has completed her final act. He releases me. I step out. The hinges on the door groan as it shuts.

The bakkie waits as the gate rolls open. The bakkie is still there as I step over the track, pressing the button to send it rolling to a close. I walk a few steps when my toe taps the soap dish that I had given to Dylan. Stooping over to pick it up, I consider the man. Will he come back? It seems likely, despite how awful we must be to work for. Then again, perhaps our oddities and seclusion makes us preferable employers to those who would hover and micromanage.

The bakkie is witnessing all of this—me, standing with a soap dish, unmoving. It would be wrong to make him think I may turn around, my mind changed. Forcing my feet forward, I ascend the steps. The door yields to a simple push without aid of key. Shutting the door, I stand and wait. Slowly I count. I've whispered fifty-seven before I hear the bakkie's grumbling departure.

The door to our bedroom is shut. I slip inside, and switch on the bedside lamp. The man between the sheets doesn't move. His complexion is that of spoilt yogurt. Eyelids are blue veined. A single bony hand peeks out from the bedding, palm out, as if begging for mercy. I smell death.

A large intake of air causes the sheets to swell. The lips smack together twice. He swallows, the Adam's apple bobbing in the pale, scrawny throat. Relief that he is alive mingles with the disappointment that things are the same. As if I expected him to have dramatically changed as a reward for my loyal return.

I depart. The door closes with a quiet click.

In the kitchen, there is nothing on the draining board to indicate that he has eaten. Nothing in the fridge has been disturbed. I locate a chilled bottle of white and remove it. As I shut the door I spot a knife lying on top of the breadbox. I walk over and peer inside. A half slice has been carved from the top, leaving a ledge in the loaf.

I shut the box and open a cabinet. I remove a solitary wine glass. Crystal. My in-laws were given it on their wedding day many years ago. My mother-in-law still owned the complete set on the day she died. Since then, I've managed to break three. Genuine accidents, after too much drink.

I make my way to the stoep, plucking a soft mohair blanket from a rocking chair and settling it over my shoulders. My husband and I purchased it during a holiday in Prince Albert. The woman in the shop informed us that the name of its colour was sea foam. I had glanced at the pale misty green and wondered if she had ever had the opportunity to see the ocean, whose crusted froth is white and grey flecked with brown grains of sand.

Stepping out into the cool night, I bypass the table and chairs, plonking myself on the steps. First glass poured, I raise it to my lips, draining it without pause for breath. The chill spreads through my veins, numbing my raw and tatty lips, hushing the weeping of my skin.

I pour a second glass. Twirling the stem between my fingertips, I admire how the liquid catches snatches of light filtering down from the night sky. Yet most of the garden is keeping its secrets tucked inside the dark. A glint here and twinkle there, peeping from shadows, perhaps keeping an eye on my huddled shape.

This is a night made for lovers.

The frogs are clicking out their own percussion, the mosquitoes swarm, doubtless plotting to make me their next meal. Yet I am alone.

I could be in Luxolo's arms at this moment. Coupled. Completely. Instead I choose this: sitting outside on the stoep step, a bottle for companionship.

Luxolo would have gladly allowed me to drink at his flat. I know it. He'd already poured me a glass. Chilled red was not the horror I would have assumed. But at the time, I had wanted him more than the drink.

It was good to walk away. Not like a wicker basket. Simply the correct choice. Not for Bart, or necessarily myself. Luxolo does not need to be saddled with a woman who would treat him as a crutch. He deserves somebody who would not use him as Bart uses me. Luxolo is a good man. Good, like a wicker basket.

There were no words to make him understand this. I'm not sure anyone can. Except, perhaps, Bart.

In the beginning of life without Kai, I ventured to the computer looking for support, people who understood. Instead I found families who turned their lives, their homes, their everything, into a museum for the baby that was lost. Then there were the families who went to the dramatic other end of the spectrum, tossing away the old and moving on, so abruptly that the child had vanished but for the hushed, anonymous typed confessions on the internet. The people in their everyday praised them for *coping so well*. Now these families felt they could not admit that the ghost of their baby had followed them to their new lives, haunting their sleep.

They say the grief never disappears; but with time some people can learn to adapt and live with grief rather than in grief.

I wish this for Bart. And myself.

This is something Luxolo, whose life still holds much promise, cannot comprehend. How it feels to have so much, and then lose it, never to have again. There can never be another Kai.

Right before we climbed into his bakkie he had asked, 'Is this really all you wish from life?'

I'd simply shaken my head, once again replying with a mixed message. I do have dreams. But they have evolved into the commonplace. How could he understand when even Old Ella would have not? That there is real value in the trivial, mundane details of the everyday.

Here is my wish: a husband, my husband, who would sit beside me contently on the stoep at the end of each day. Together in companionable silence, we'd watch the changing light of eventide. On Fridays, or maybe a Saturday or a Sunday, we would hold braais. Gatherings without drama: some laughter, a spilled drink here or there, a dollop of chutney on the chin, while the citronella candles burned without noticeable effect.

After the guests departed, Bart and I would only clean up what was absolutely necessary. The rest would be left for another day. We would curl up with one final drink, chatting about our friends, life. Then we would put our glasses down. He'd give me a kiss. We'd make broken love, but together.

My wish.

Luxolo offered me another path: mere moments, no hope for a future. He has no concept of how damaged I truly am. At first he would take care of me, as if I were a wounded bird. I would take and take with nothing to give, until disgust would eventually drive me to run away. The relationship would merely be an exhilarating tipping point, spinning me off in a direction far from here.

But what truly hurts would stalk me, wherever I fled. My boy is neither here, nor somewhere else, yet fully present everywhere, hollowing me out. Today proved that.

Bart, I could leave entirely. Eventually. Perhaps he'd slough off gradually, like layers of skin. They say it takes a full seven years for the epidermis to regenerate. Perhaps the we that was us is doing exactly that. Slowly regenerating into new selves, one without the other. Perhaps he is simply waiting for me to leave, so he can complete the metamorphosis.

Not yet.

I still crave those braais.

There remains a longing for the man I know he could be. Not the same, of course. After all, Old Ella is gone too. You cannot go back. But it *must* be possible for New Bart to be better than *this* Bart.

Or so I hope.

I think.

New doctor, perhaps.

Second glass empty, I slip into the house, returning to my husband's side. He's still breathing. A line of drool is etching its way down his chin.

Climbing between the sheets, I curl up against his slumbering husk. As the light goes out, I utter a silent plea for sleep to come.

This is my day. I have nothing more to give. Tomorrow I will go down to the beach and write to Kai as the sun rises from the sea.

Sunrise: 5:27am.

I will stand there at the ocean's edge and wait for the water to devour my words.

Low tide: 6:03am.

This is what the pamphlet says. That is what will happen.

Every day we begin again.

THANK YOU:

A lot of people like to believe they are self-made, their accomplishments their own. Living with chronic conditions wipes away any such delusion. This book is a team effort created on a dirt road filled with potholes. How many people? A list longer than is appropriate to print. So I give you the highly edited version of thanks:

Thank you to my parents and countless relatives who instilled in me the love of books. Thank you to my family: The Things and a Husband who puts up with me – constructing an office or workspace wherever we go. To my friends, near and far, who have cheered me on and have done more favours than I can ever repay. To the RSA writing community (and beyond) for accepting me even though I often felt I shouldn't belong. This includes my local writing group who has listened not only to my countless drafts, but my vents. Also a thank you to anyone who has supported Short Story Day Africa either by giving their time or funds – your enthusiasm feeds into mine.

Thank you to every person who has ever published my work. Thank you to all my past editors who acknowledge the art of my prose while patiently – tirelessly – guiding me through the craft of writing, including: Rose Malinaric, Moira Richards, Andie Miller, Helen Brain and Helen Moffett. To Louis Greenberg for kindly answering my panicked emails with advice. To Sarah Lotz for reading the book and giving encouragement. Thank you to Rachel Zadok who not only proved to me I wasn't useless, but also read this book and refused to allow it to rot on my desk. This wouldn't have been published without you. To Julie Bracker, my loyal steadfast friend, who has done more than words can express, including refusing to allow me to give up hope.

Thank you to Colleen Higgs who was willing to consider such a book. Thank you to Karen Jennings for being willing to bend her very tight schedule to comply with the oddities of my health in order to edit this work.

But there are two women in my life without whom I could not write. Thank you to Professor Celie Eales who refused to give up searching for ways for me to cope, to live my life, even when I was so scared I was losing the ability to type. Lastly, but not least, thank you Ntombizodwa Kokwe who has loyally seen me through my ever changing circumstances, despite her own life's stumbling blocks. Over the years I've had to cut back on many things, and you have been there, picking up the slack, keeping my family and household running smoothly when I cannot. If I had been left to do it all on my own, my writing would have ceased.

If you would like to know more about **MODJAJI** BOOKS and our other titles please visit our website at www.modjajibooks.co.za